VC ATTACK!

Heavy rifle fire poured out of the surrounding jungle into the ranks of the Black Eagles. The attack was U-shaped and almost had Falconi and his men outflanked. Within seconds, heavy automatic weapons joined in to support the enemy riflemen, whoever they were.

"Alpha! Bravo! Withdraw!" Falconi shouted into his radio.

The outfit formed up in the hellish confusion and returned fire. It was pitifully weak in comparison to the amount they were receiving.

"Bug out!" ordered Falconi.

Everyone except the Falcon and his squad leaped to their feet and ran to the rear as Falconi's troops threw out a hailstorm of fire. The first VCs, anxious but unfortunate, stumbled into the initial swarm of .556 slugs, toppling to the ground. The Reds behind them, though, kept right on coming. There were too many for Falconi . . . way too many. . . .

THE BLACK EAGLES
by John Lansing

#7
BEYOND THE DMZ

THE BLACK EAGLES

BY JOHN LANSING

ZEBRA BOOKS
KENSINGTON PUBLISHING CORP.

ZEBRA BOOKS

are published by

Kensington Publishing Corp.
475 Park Avenue South
New York, NY 10016

First printing: June 1985

Printed in the United States of America

*Dedicated to
a couple of good army buddies
Schmedlap and Nerdlinger*

Special acknowledgement to Patrick E. Andrews

AUTHOR'S NOTE

The Ping-Yan-Uen people in this book are fictitious. They are, however, based on bands of Chinese mercenaries who have plied their deadly trade as hired men-at-arms in Asia for generations. They worship former captains and generals, fighting for money and glory as their forefathers have done for centuries as followers of independent warlords.

THE BLACK EAGLES ROLE OF HONOR

(Assigned or Attached Personnel Killed in Action)

1Lt. Blum, Marc—United States Air Force
Sgt. Boudreau, Marcel—United States Army
Sgt. Carter, Demond—United States Army
S.Sgt. Dayton, Marvin—United States Army
Sfc. Galchaser, Jack—United States Army
Sgt. Hodges, Trent—United States Army
Mr. Hosteins, Bruno—ex-French Foreign Legion
PO2 Jackson, Fred—United States Navy
CPO Jenkins, Claud—United States Navy
Sgt. Limo, Raymond—United States Army
PO3 Littleton, Michael—United States Navy
Sfc. Miskoski, Jan—United States Army
S.Sgt. Newcomb, Thomas—Australian Army
1Lt. Nguyen Van Dow—Army of the Republic of
                                    Vietnam
S.Sgt. O'Quinn, Liam—United States Marine Corps
Sfc. Ormond, Norman—United States Army
Sgt. Park, Chun Ri—Republic of Korea Marines
Sfc. Rivera, Manuel—United States Army
M.Sgt. Snow, John—United States Army
Lt. Thompson, William—United States Navy
1Lt. Wakely, Richard—United States Army
S.Sgt. Whitaker, George—Australian Army

ROSTER OF THE BLACK EAGLES
(*Operation Guerrilla Hell*)

Maj. Robert Falconi
United States Army
Commanding Officer

M.Sgt. Duncan Gordon
United States Army
Operations Sergeant

M.Sgt. Chun Kim
Republic of Korea Marines
Heavy Weapons

Sfc. Calvin Culpepper
United States Army
Demolitions Sergeant

Sfc. Malcomb McCorckel
United States Army
Medic

Sfc. Ray Swift Elk
United States Army
Intelligence Sergeant

S.Sgt. Archibald Dobbs
United States Army
Detachment Scout

PO, 2c Durwood Martin
United States Navy
Radio Operator

S.Sgt. Dennis Maywood
United States Army
Light Weapons

S.Sgt. Charlie Tripper
United States Army
Supply Sergeant

Sgt. Toby Barker
United States Marine Corps
Light Weapons

PO, 3c Blue Richards
United States Navy
Demolitions

PROLOGUE

The soldiers were drawn up in perfect formation in front of the village's largest hut. The jungle, hot and misty, pressed in relentlessly toward the hamlet. Only the inhabitants' machetes, wielded daily, kept the encroaching vegetation at bay.

The men's uniforms, while clean, were nondescript and varied from individual to individual. A couple of the more fortunate ones sported leather boots, but some had to make do with canvas leggings and sandals. There was even an older man who sported split-toed Japanese jungle shoes dating from World War II.

Despite their appearance, their well-ordered ranks and serious demeanors gave stark evidence they were a highly disciplined group.

Off to the side, keeping themselves respectfully silent, their women and children watched the solemn ceremony that was about to begin.

These people called themselves the Ping-Yan-Uen. Of Chinese descent, they had been away from the nation of their origins for ten generations. In fact, they had forgotten the old country entirely, having only their language and strange customs to remind them that they were very different from the other peoples of Indochina.

11

The *foo-koon*, who had been standing behind the men, walked around to the front and clapped his hands three distinct, separate times, the sound deadened by the heavy rain forest around them.

Every adult male bowed deeply and reverently, and the women and children went down on their knees, their eyes respectfully downcast.

The figure of a man appeared from another nearby hut. He was dressed as a soldier, but certainly not a modern one. He wore heavily lacquered breastplate made of wood and carried a curved Chinese sword called a *shou-tao*. The rest of his attire was made up of a silk robe, while a skull cap bearing ancient designs was set on the back of his head. A closer inspection of the costume would have revealed it to be an authentic antique garb hundreds of years old.

He strode through a prearranged path in the formation of soldiers up to the *foo-koon*. The two bowed to each other, then the armored man ascended a short ladder up to the porch of the larger hut. He stopped and turned to face the assembled people. He raised his hands in a gesture so lost in antiquity that none were sure of its true meaning anymore.

After repeating the movement three distinct times, he backed slowly into the interior of the crude building.

This man's name was Tsang, and he was the leader of the Ping-Yan-Uen people. He walked to a small altar and knelt before it. The religious device, like the attire he wore, was also ancient, having been the property of the Ping-Yan-Uen for countless generations. It was painted black with several Chinese characters written across it. The badly faded figure of a Chinese warrior of some long-ago dynasty was painted on the center of the back board.

Tsang removed the sword, scabbard and all, and laid it reverently across the altar. Then, after lighting sticks of incense, he clapped his hands three times and called out,

"Pyang Tseung! Pyang Tseung!"

He put his hands together in a prayerful attitude and touched them to his forehead. After closing his eyes, he sat there for several minutes before slowly bending forward until his face was almost touching the floor.

Tsang maintained the difficult position for more than an hour. Yet he felt no discomfort as he drifted off into a trance that made him oblivious to his surroundings. He was absolutely still except for an occasional twitch, as he maintained the deep meditative prayer.

Suddenly he sat up, and his eyes popped open. He lowered his hands to his side, staring at the altar. A few minutes more and he stood up, retrieving the sword at the same time. Tsang walked slowly to the door of the hut and out onto the porch to face the assembled soldiers and their families.

An old woman carrying a cup filled with strong tea scurried forward to him. Tsang gulped the brew down, then took a deep breath to further help him recover from the trance he had just been in. Then he spoke in a loud voice. "I have spoken to the great Pyang Tseung," he announced, "and he has given me his answer."

The *foo-koon* stepped forward. "What has he told you, Tsang *Sheung-Wai*?"

Tsang pulled the sword from the scabbard and held it high above his head. "Pyang Tseung has told us to fight for the Americans!"

The solemnity of the occasion disintegrated immediately. The Ping-Yan-Uen, their Oriental faces creased with happy smiles, shouted their joy at the news.

"Gaaung-Po! Gaaung-Po! Gaaung-Po!"

They would soon be deeply involved in their favorite pastime: war.

13

CHAPTER ONE

Maj. Robert Falconi, accompanied by an MP escort, walked through the hall of MAC V SOG headquarters. This building, located at Peterson Air Field in Saigon, was heavily guarded, with the interior as closely watched as the exterior. Here was located the brains of several ultrasecret projects that were designed to break the back of the Communist insurgency in Southeast Asia.

The extent of security arrangements inside the building was evidenced not only by the close eye the MP guard kept on Falconi, but also because of the number of checkpoints at which the two men were forced to stop and properly identify themselves.

The major, although a well-known and proven commander of a number of dangerous clandestine forays behind enemy lines, was not allowed to be in any part of the edifice without proper escort or credentials.

Falconi, a step or two ahead of the guard, knew where he was going. He ascended the stairs to the second floor and turned down the hallway until he reached a far door. He waited for the MP to rap on the heavy portal. A feminine voice, distorted slightly by the electronics, spoke out from a speaker on the wall.

"Yes? Identification, please."

"The Falcon," the MP said. Then he took a plastic card he had been carrying and slipped it into a slot. Within moments the voice spoke again. "The ID is correct."

There was a short buzz, then a click before the door popped open a bit. Falconi nodded his thanks to the guard, then stepped through.

Lt. Andrea Thuy, the beautiful administrative assistant to CIA case officer Chuck Fagin, smiled a delighted welcome to the caller. "Robert! So nice to see you again."

Falconi embraced her and gave her a brotherly kiss on the cheek. "How've you been, Andrea?"

"I am fine, thank you, Robert," she replied.

Falconi let his eyes enjoy the sight before him. Andrea, an officer in the South Vietnamese Army, was a striking Eurasian woman. She had been on several operations in enemy territory, and, despite her undeniable feminine qualities, was a trained and experienced soldier.

"I wish we had time for a short chat," Andrea said. "But Fagin is in a big hurry to see you." She walked to an inner door and opened it. "He's in a bit of a hurry."

Falconi laughed. "Then I'd better not keep him waiting. It's too early in the day to have the wrath of a pissed-off Irishman descend on me."

"Good thinking," Andrea answered.

Falconi entered the office and found himself facing a stocky, dark man looking at him from over an incredibly cluttered desk. Falconi nodded to him. "How's it going, Fagin?"

Chuck Fagin rubbed a hand through the small bit of black hair on his head and emitted a sigh of relief. "Thank God you're not late." He offered his hand.

"What's going on?" Falconi asked. "You and Andrea seem to be in some kind of sweat."

"We are," Fagin said. "A recent situation, really a godsend to our side, has surfaced. We want to take advantage of it before it slips away."

16

Falconi, curious, took a seat. "Well, don't keep me in suspense, pal."

"Right. Are you familiar with the Ping-Yan-Uen?"

Falconi thought for a moment. "Uh—yeah, I think so. They're a bunch of Chinese bandits, if my memory serves me right."

"You're partially correct," Fagin said lighting a cigar. "They're Chinese all right, but they're not exactly a *bunch of bandits,* as you put it. They're a highly developed, independent society of mercenary soldiers."

"Sometimes, particularly in Asia, there's damned little difference between bandits and mercenaries," Falconi said. "One man's warlord is another's robber baron."

"Certainly," Fagin said. "Not unlike one man's freedom fighter being another's terrorist. And I'm sure the Ping-Yan-Uen have done their share of looting and raping. But their approach to it is a bit more sophisticated than you'd imagine."

"I'd have to go back through old notes and books to see what I have on them," Falconi said. "But it wouldn't be much."

Fagin took a drag off the cigar. "They're the descendents of a group of followers who were once devoted to an ancient Chinese warlord. God only knows how far back they go. Their entire culture is based on fighting, and that includes their religion."

"Sort of like they're Oriental vikings worshiping their own kind of Odin, huh?"

"Yeah," Fagin said. "Except they pray to the souls of their dead generals for advice and guidance. If their decisions, based on those prayers, turn out well, they feel the old dead brass hats are pleased with them and are helping."

"What if everything goes to hell for them?" Falconi asked.

"Then they think the old generals are mad at them,

and they make sacrifices and perform other purification ceremonies—and try again."

"Not human sacrifices, I hope," Falconi mused aloud.

"Nope. Pigs."

Falconi laughed. "In other words, their motto is—'If at first you don't succeed, butcher a pig.'"

"That's it," Fagin said displaying a grin. "At any rate, we've had an indigenous operative in their area for some time trying to recruit them to our cause. We've been working with their leader, who is a real tough character by the name of Tsang. Or, to use his proper title, Tsang *Sheung-Wai*—Captain Tsang."

"Only a captain?"

"Yeah. According to their religion you don't make general until you die," Fagin explained. "The highest rank for mere mortals is captain."

"And, after dying, they not only make general but get prayed to, right?"

"Right," Fagin said. "You become an instant saint upon your departure from the woes and cares of this mortal world."

Falconi laughed. "I suppose if one of 'em gets killed by artillery, he's considered canonized by cannon, right?"

Fagin sighed aloud at the poor joke. "Jesus!"

"Sorry about that," Falconi said. "Anyhow, it sounds great." He made himself more comfortable by stretching out his legs. "I presume you're not enlightening me about the Ping-Yan-Uen in order to simply further my education. Am I right in assuming that the Black Eagles will be the first to work with these mercenaries?"

"Again you're correct," Fagin said. "But the operation is going to be a bit hairy, I'm afraid."

"Jesus, Fagin!" Falconi exclaimed. "Will you please tell me of one time you haven't gotten us into something that didn't cause nervous perspiration?"

"This time the danger factor is going to be multiplied

18

by certain attitudes of your new allies," Fagin said. "You might have already figured out the problem. Since getting killed in battle means sainthood to these jokers, they—"

"They don't mind dying," Falconi interrupted, finishing the sentence. "And that means there's a good chance they might drag us into their form of immortality."

"They're good soldiers," Fagin said. "But they can turn into bloodthirsty, undisciplined warriors in the twinkling of an eye."

"Oh, well," Falconi said with a sigh. "I never figured anything about this job would be easy."

Fagin displayed a wry smile. "Well, I'm glad I'm not disappointing you."

"When does this operation start?"

"Yesterday," Fagin answered. "We'll move you and your boys into Isolation immediately. You should be out into the cold within forty-eight hours."

Falconi got to his feet. "Well—as the old cowboy said—I'd better go round up the herd."

Maj. Robert Falconi was the commanding officer of a unique detachment known as the Black Eagles. This small command, attached to Special Operations Group of MAC V, was under the direct supervision of the Central Intelligence Agency through Chuck Fagin, a CIA case officer. Fagin's experience in clandestine warfare went back to working with Yugoslavian partisans in World War II, and he thought he had seen everything when it came to conducting secret missions that penetrated deep into enemy territory. But there in South Vietnam he found danger lurking back in the friendly areas, too.

The Black Eagles were still pretty much a new organization despite the amount of action they had seen. Their first efforts had been directed against a pleasure palace in North Vietnam. This bordello *par excellence* was used by Communist officials during their retreats from the trials and tribulations of administering authority and regulation over their slave populations. There were no excesses, perverted tastes, or unusual demands that went unsatisfied in this hidden fleshpot.

Falconi and his wrecking crew sky-dived into the operational area in a HALO (High Altitude Low Opening) infiltration, and when the Black Eagles finished their raid on the whorehouse, there was hardly a soul left alive to continue the debauchery.

Their next hell-trek into the enemy's hinterlands was an even more dangerous assignment with the difficulty factor multiplied by the special demands placed on them. The North Vietnamese had set up a special prison camp in which they were perfecting their skills in the torture-interrogation of downed American pilots. With the conflict escalating in Southeast Asia, they rightly predicted they would soon have more than a few Yanks in their hands. A North Korean brainwashing expert had come over from his native country to teach them the fine points of mental torment. He had learned his despicable trade during the Korean War when he had American POWs directly under his control. His use of psychological torture, combined with just the right amount of physical torment, had broken more than one man despite the most spirited resistance. Experts who studied his methods came to the conclusion that only a completely insane prisoner could have resisted the North Korean's methods.

At the time of the Black Eagles' infiltration into North Vietnam, the prisoners behind the barbed wire were few—but important. A U.S.A.F. pilot, an army Special Forces sergeant, and two high-ranking officers of the South Vietnamese forces were the unwilling tenants of the concentration camp.

Falconi and his men were not only tasked to rescue the POWs but also had to bring along the prison's commandant and that North Korean tutor. Falconi pulled the job off, fighting his way south through the North Vietnamese army and air force to a bloody showdown on the Song Bo River. The situation deteriorated to the point that the Black Eagles' magazines had their last few rounds in them as they waited for the NVA's final charge.

The next operation took them to Laos where they were pitted against the fanatical savages of the Pathet Lao. If that wasn't bad enough, their method of entrance into the operational area was bizarre and dangerous. This type of transport into battle hadn't been used in active combat in more than twenty years. It had even been labeled obsolete by the military experts. But this didn't deter the Black Eagles from the idea.

They used a glider to make a silent flight to a secret landing zone. If that wasn't bad enough, the operations plan called for their extraction through a glider-recovery apparatus that had never been tested in combat.

After a hairy ride in the flimsy craft, they hit the ground to carry out a mission designed to destroy the construction site of a Soviet nuclear power plant the Reds wanted to install in the area. Everything went wrong from the start, and the Black Eagles fought against a horde of insane zealots until their extraction to safety. This was completely dependent on the illegal and unauthorized efforts of a dedicated U.S.A.F. pilot—the same one they had rescued from the North Vietnam prison camp. The air force colonel was determined to help the same men who had saved him, but many times even the deadliest determination isn't enough.

All this had taken place in 1964, and they wrapped up that year with a mission that had been doubly dangerous because of an impossibility to make firm operational plans. Unknown Caucasian personnel, posing as U.S. troops, had been committing atrocities against Vietnamese peasants. The situation had gotten far enough out of control that the effectiveness of American efforts in the area had been badly damaged. Once again Falconi and the Black Eagles were called upon to sort things out. They went in on a dark beach from a submarine and began a deadly reconnaissance until they finally made contact with their quarry. These enemy agents, wearing U.S. Army uniforms, were dedicated East German Communists prepared to fight to the death for their cause. The Black Eagles admired such unselfish dedication to the extent that they gave the Reds the opportunity to accomplish that end—give their lives for Communism. But this wasn't accomplished without the situation deteriorating to the point the Black Eagles had to endure human wave assaults from a North Vietnamese army battalion led by an infuriated general. This officer had been humiliated by Falconi on the Song Bo River several months previously. The mission ended in another Black Eagle victory—but not before five more men had died.

Brought back to Saigon at last, the seven survivors of the previous operations had cleaned their weapons, drawn fresh, clean uniforms and prepared for a long awaited period of R&R.

It was not to be.

Chuck Fagin's instincts and organization of agents had ferreted out information that showed a high-ranking intelligence officer of the South Vietnamese army had been leaking information on the Black Eagles to his superiors up in the Communist north. It would have been easy enough to arrest this double agent, but an entire enemy espionage net had been involved. Thus, Falconi and his Black Eagles had to come in from the boondocks and fight the good fight against these spies and assassins in the back streets and alleys of Saigon itself.

22

Their last mission had involved going out on the Ho Chi Minh trail on which the North Vietnamese sent supplies, weapons, and munitions south to be used by the Viet Cong and elements of the North Vietnamese army. The enemy was enjoying great success despite repeated aerial attacks by the U.S. and South Vietnam air forces. The high command decided that only a sustained campaign conducted on the ground would put a crimp in the Reds' operation.

Naturally, they chose the Black Eagles for the dirty and dangerous job.

Falconi and his men waged partisan warfare in its most primitive and violent fashion with raids, ambushes, and other forms of jungle fighting. The order of the day was "kill or be killed" as the rain forest thundered with reports of numerous types of modern weaponry, while the more insidious and deadly forms of mine warfare made each track and trail through the brush a potential zone of death.

Now, with hardly a breather, because of the sudden recruitment of a group of Chinese mercenaries, Falconi and company would soon be back into the war.

This time on a mission the big planners upstairs had labeled Operation Guerrilla Hell.

CHAPTER TWO

There was a part of each Black Eagles mission known as *Isolation*, and the label was most appropriate.

The members of the team were virtually isolated from the rest of the world as they did the skull work—combined with a bit of fetching and coordination—required to prepare themselves for the upcoming operation.

During Isolation they were thoroughly briefed in all aspects of the scheduled mission. Each man, according to his specialty, was steeped in every known bit of information regarding plans, weaponry, intelligence, commo, contingencies, etc. until he could recite them frontward and backward, not only in English but also in whatever language he had acquired during his highly specialized training.

Cut off from liquor, women, and all good times while being kept under guard, they worked long and hard at absorbing all they were expected to learn. Even their meals were brought in to them, and their trash and garbage was thoroughly searched before being transported to the proper disposal facilities.

The only men allowed to leave Isolation were the commander and others who had legitimate errands pertaining to the mission. This would generally be the supply sergeant who always had some equipment to pick up, or the intelligence NCO who was required to keep himself updated at all times on happenings within the proposed operational area.

After learning their own particular missions, the men were expected to brief the other detachment members and the CIA case officer Chuck Fagin, in a phase of Isolation called the briefback. This activity doubled the demands on the men, for now they had to learn the other guys' jobs, too.

It was all right to be dumb enough to do dangerous things in order to become a Black Eagle, but not dumb enough where you couldn't learn—and learn fast!

The MP checked their IDs, then opened the door and admitted Chuck Fagin and Andrea Thuy into the inner sanctum of the Black Eagles' Isolation Area.

Fagin noted the arrangement of chairs, the blackboard, and map of the operational area. "Looks like they're ready for the briefback."

"Seems so," Andrea acknowledged. She preceded him to a couple of chairs toward the back of the room. Andrea checked her watch. "They should be coming in shortly."

"Yeah," Fagin said. "Make yourself comfortable, I'd like to meet them at the door. The only guy I've seen lately is the Falcon."

He had no sooner spoken than Major Falconi stepped into the room. The officer wore the standard uniform of the Black Eagles: tiger-striped camouflaged fatigues without insignia. The Falcon seemed extraordinarily solemn as he stood there, darkly handsome, staring rather ominously out of his sea-green eyes. Six feet one inch tall and a tight, muscular one hundred and ninety-five pounds, he walked with an easy grace.

26

Fagin approached him. "Nice to see you again, Falconi. How do things look?"

"The detachment is shaped up and ready to roll," Falconi said. "The boys have been picking each other's brains, so I'd say they're more than ready for the briefback." He waved a greeting to Andrea, then went to the front of the room to wait for the rest of the men. Fagin stationed himself by the door in order to give each Black Eagle a handshake as they entered.

The next man to come into the debriefing room was M.Sgt. Duncan "Top" Gordon, the senior noncommissioned officer of the Black Eagles. His position required several tasks. Besides forming the operation plans for the missions, he was also responsible for maintaining discipline and efficiency within the unit. A husky man, his jet-black hair was thinning perceptively, looking even more sparse because of the strict GI haircut he wore.

Gordon's entrance into the Black Eagles had been less than satisfactory. After seventeen years spent in the army's elite spit-and-polish airborne infantry units, he had brought in an attitude that did not fit well into the diverse individuals in Falconi's command. Gordon's zeal to follow army regulations to the letter had cost him a marriage, but he hadn't let up a bit. To make things worse, he had taken the place of a popular detachment sergeant who was killed in action on the Song Bo River. This noncom, called "Top" by the men, was an old Special Forces man who knew how to handle the type of soldier volunteering for unconventional units. Gordon's first day in his new assignment brought him into quick conflict with the Black Eagle personnel that soon got so far out of hand that Falconi began to seriously consider relieving the sergeant and seeing to his transfer back to a regular airborne unit.

But during Operation Laos Nightmare, Gordon's bravery under fire earned him the grudging respect of the lower ranking Black Eagles. Finally, when he fully realized the problems he had created for himself, he changed his methods of leadership. Gordon backed off doing things by the book and found he could still maintain good discipline and efficiency while getting rid of the chicken-shit aspects of army life. It was most apparent he had been accepted by the men when they bestowed the nickname "Top" on him. He had truly become the "top sergeant" then.

The next man to enter the debriefing area was a short, stocky South Korean marine sergeant named Chun Kim. Kim, a heavy weapons infantry expert and third degree black belt in Tai Kwan Do karate, had been serving continuously in the military since 1948. His experience ran the gamut from the poorly trained and equipped South Korea armed forces that melted under the Communist onslaught from the north in June of 1950, to the later highly motivated and superbly disciplined elite marines created in the years after the cease-fire.

Kim was followed by Sfc. Calvin Culpepper. This tall, brawny black man had entered the army off a poor Georgia farm his family worked as sharecroppers. He handled the explosive chores that popped up from time to time. It was said he could set a C4 plastic charge under a silver dollar and get back fifty cents in change. Ten years of dedicated service in the United States Army had produced an excellent soldier. Resourceful and combat-wise, Calvin pulled his weight—and then a bit more—in the dangerous undertakings of the Black Eagles.

The detachment medic, Sfc. Malcomb "Malpractice" McCorckel, came in on Calvin's heels. An inch under six feet in height, Malpractice had been in the army for twelve years. He had a friendly face and spoke softly as he pursued his duties in seeing after the illnesses and hurts of his buddies. He nagged and needled them in his efforts

28

to keep the wild bunch healthy. They bitched back at him for his mother-hen attitude, but each Black Eagle appreciated his concern. They all knew that nothing devised by puny man could keep Malpractice from reaching a wounded detachment member and pulling him back to safety.

Sfc. Ray Swift Elk was given the unit's intelligence work. A full-blooded Sioux Indian from South Dakota, he was lean and muscular. His copper-colored skin, prominent nose, and high cheek bones gave him the appearance of the classic prairie warrior. With twelve years of service, he was well experienced in his job.

The man with the most dangerous job in the detachment was S.Sgt. Archie Dobbs. As point man and scout, he went into dangerous areas first, just to see what—or who—was there. Reputed to be the best compass man in the United States Army, his seven years of service was fraught with stints in the stockade and dozens of "busts" to lower rank. Fond of women, pot, and booze, Archie's claim to fame—and object of genuine respect from the other men—was that he had saved their asses on more than one occasion by guiding them safely through throngs of enemy troops while behind enemy lines.

One of the United States Navy's contributions to the Black Eagles made his entrance. A radioman second class, PO Durwood Martin was a short, husky man with hair as black as Swift Elk's. A veteran of the SEALS, his skin was as fair as a teen-age maiden's. But it didn't match his murderous face. He was called "Sparks" because of navy tradition regarding his military specialty in communications.

The group was joined by S.Sgt. Dennis Maywood. He was a diminutive man who had barely passed the army's minimum height and weight requirements. He was on his second tour in Vietnam (he had also had one in Laos in the late 1950s), and he sported the silver star with cluster.

Despite his small size, Maywood had a deep, resounding voice completely out of character with his physical appearance. It didn't take the others long to dub him "Bullhorn" because of his amazing ability to be able to make himself heard farther than the brassiest sergeant major.

S.Sgt. Charlie Tripper, the detachment supply sergeant, joined his comrades-in-arms. The Tripper had nearly eighteen years in the army. He was rotund to the point his physical conditioning was suspect, but he always managed to pass the toughest PT tests. His face, a bit blotched and ruddy, showed evidence of its owner's habit of imbibing hard liquor in large quantities. As a supply NCO he was known to carry enough surplus to equip units three and four times the size of his own. Yet the sharpest inspector generals had never been able to discover as much as an extra paper clip during the many hours they'd spent pouring over his property books and searching the nooks and crannies of his equipment bins. He was reputed to be one of the most creative men with paperwork in the United States Armed Forces.

An extremely muscular young marine made his appearance. Sgt. Toby Barker was an infantry light weapons specialist. He was a clean-cut kid with five years of service. He looked like he should be playing football at Notre Dame rather than being a professional fighting man, but Toby was doing exactly what he wanted.

The final man was another SEAL. PO Blue Richards was an Alabaman who had been named after his "daddy's favorite huntin' dawg." An expert in demolitions—either on land or under water—Blue considered himself honored for his father to have given him that dog's name.

Falconi waited for the men to settle down. After

spending the last two days together in Isolation, they weren't in much of a mood for a lot of conversation with each other, so they engaged in no unnecessary chatting.

"Okay, listen up," the major said. "It's briefback time, and the sooner we get into it the better. We aren't exactly brimming with excess time on this operation. So listen up and absorb the data. Your life, your buddies' lives, and *my* life depends on it. As usual, I'll start the auspicious occasion by announcing our mission."

The Black Eagles, though aware of what they had been assigned to do, unconsciously leaned forward to get the official word.

"Our mission is to make a parachute infiltration into Operational Area Bravo." He put his finger at place on map. "Which is located here in the northwest part of South Vietnam between Kontum and the Laotian border." He turned back to his subordinates. "Once there, we are to link up with a Chinese mercenary group known as the Ping-Yan-Uen—or the 'Pings,' as you guys have started calling them. We'll form a combined unit to conduct counterinsurgency operations against the Viet Cong unit which is active in that territory. Due to special circumstances, the brass figure we'll be able to completely pacify the OA within a matter of weeks. Are there any questions regarding what SOG wants of us?" He waited, and when there were none, he said, "Top Gordon, as the operations sergeant, will give you the execution phase of the briefback."

Top strode to the front of the room as Falconi took a seat off to one side. The master sergeant faced the detachment. "You are now at D minus one. This, of course, means that tomorrow is when we'll be committed to the operation. The infiltration phase, by T10 parachute out of the South Vietnamese air force C-123 will be as follows. We'll have an early reveille in Isolation at oh one forty-five hours. Chow will be oh two-thirty.

31

We're giving you that forty-five minutes to make doubly sure all your equipment is there and ready to go. Be damned sure you check it before you hit the sack. Anybody that's fucked up—is going to get *fucked up.* Understood? Draw chutes at the SOG hangar here at Peterson Field at oh three-fifteen hours. We'll immediately chute-up and have rigger and jumpmaster checks. Station time is oh three forty-five and takeoff is scheduled for oh four hundred. Drop time is oh five hundred at this DZ." He turned to the map and indicated the place with a pointer. "Believe it or not, it's a thirty-second drop zone thanks to a series of abandoned rice paddies."

"Rice paddies!" Archie Dobbs yelled.

Top grinned. "Yeah. We'll have wet landings."

"And muddy," Calvin Culpepper added.

"Right," Top said. "And that means to look out for the nearest guy after you've landed. If you see he's been injured and is in danger of drowning or suffocating in the mud, pull him out. And don't waste time indicating that you're okay, if you're okay."

"What if we're completely under the water?" Archie Dobbs asked.

"Blow bubbles, baby!" Calvin hollered. "We'll find you!"

"How'm I gonna blow bubbles with my face stuck in the muddy bottom of a rice paddy?" Archie demanded.

"Fart, man fart!" Calvin said laughing.

Top grinned. "Good thinking, Calvin. After the jump, the link up with the Pings should be accomplished by oh five-fifteen. At that time we'll move off with them to their base camp, where we shall, as our fearless leader said, 'conduct counterinsurgency operations against the Viet Cong in the area.'"

Toby Barker, the marine, raised his hand. "Any particular activities laid on at this time, Top?"

Gordon shook his head. "No. We'll play it by ear. Any intel we've got now will be outdated. The Pings are a bunch of active little guys and will give us the latest poop. The Falcon and I will work out future operations with their honcho. Now I'll turn the floor over to Ray Swift Elk for the intelligence portion of this event."

Top returned to his seat and passed the Sioux on his way to the front. "Like the operations sergeant said, we don't know a hell of a lot about what the latest situation is," Swift Elk said. "But I'll give you what SOGs have been able to dig up for us."

Archie Dobbs raised his hand. "Are there women with these here Pings? And, if so, are they good lookin' enough to deserve my personal attention?"

Blue Richards laughed outloud. "Shit-far, Archie, boy! My daddy's got sows in the pen behind the barn that're too damn good for the likes o' you!"

Falconi interrupted. "You leave the Ping women alone, Archie. Those people have high moral standards and messing with their ladies will bring their righteous wrath down on you."

"Yes, sir," Archie said. Then he turned and glared at Blue. "I reckon I'm good enough for your daddy's sows—" Then he realized what he'd said. "I mean your daddy's sows ain't—"

"Shut up while you're ahead, Archie," Top Gordon said.

Archie wisely took the master sergeant's advice.

"Let's talk about the Pings—or, as their real name is—the Ping-Yan-Uen," Swift Elk said. "They're of Chinese ancestry, and they've been hiring out as mercenary soldiers here and abouts in different parts of Indochina for several generations. They are a highly moral—" He glanced at Archie. "Incredibly brave bunch of little guys. They're absolutely fearless, because of their religion."

Sparks Martin lit a cigarette. "Am I right in assumin'

33

they ain't Presbyterians?"

"You are," Swift Elk said. "They have a rather simple belief that they are guided and advised by the spirits of their dead generals. They pray to these saints whenever they have questions or problems. They also believe that when they die, they will become saints."

"Oh, brother!" Archie Dobbs exclaimed. "So every war they fight in is a holy war."

"Well put," Swift Elk said. "That means we'll have to keep them under as tight rein as possible. If we don't, they're going to go crazy and get us all listed on the casualty rosters." He took a deep breath and slowly exhaled. "Guys, them little bastards love combat, and they figure their dead generals are gonna help 'em out. I ain't got that much faith in their style o' worship, so let me repeat. Be careful and don't go gallopin' off somewheres just 'cause some Ping thinks it's a good idea."

Malpractice McCorckel had a question. "Is that all we know about their culture?"

"That's it," Swift Elk said with a shrug. "But don't worry, we'll all be experts on 'em before this operation is over. There is one positive thing, though. They speak a pretty good brand of English."

"How did that come about?" Calvin asked.

"They served in World War II with British and American forces, Buffalo Soljer," Swift Elk explained. "Their brand of our lingo ain't the best, but we'll be able to understand each other."

"I just hope this holy war ideals o' theirs don't get outta hand," Archie Dobbs said. "We could end up in some deep shit."

"Keep that in mind," Swift Elk said. "Now let's turn our collective attention to Charlie out there. G2 tells me they're about a two-comp'ny size unit and pretty well equipped. They're a bit goosey about the Pings from havin' fought 'em before, so we do have a big advantage there. Charlie has demonstrated he'll run from 'em, so some real careful enveloping actions are gonna have to be worked out."

"Hey, them kind of operations are hairy and dangerous," Calvin Culpepper said.

"Sure are, Buffalo Soljer," Swift Elk replied. "But that's the only way we'll catch 'em."

"Jesus!" Archie Dobbs said. "Takin' crazy little bastards like the Pings into action like that is gonna pucker a few assholes."

"It sure as hell will," Swift Elk said. "But they're damn good, and have the VC on the run out there. That's why the brass figures we can have the area completely pacified in a relative short time. Then our guys and the ARVN will set up some fortified hamlets in the place, and it'll belong to the good guys for keeps." He paused for a moment. "Any questions?"

"Yeah," Blue Richards said. "How's come you keep callin' ol' Calvin Buffalo Soljer? You been doin' that all through this here Isolation."

"My ancestors referred to the Black cavalrymen they fought in the Indian Wars as Buffalo Soljers," Swift Elk said. "It was on account o' their hair bein' like them animals' fur. And from the reverence us Plains Indians have for the American Bison, I can assure you it was a compliment."

"Right on!" Calvin said.

"Anything else?" Swift Elk asked. "No? Okay, that's the end of the intelligence briefing. I'll turn you over to the Tripper for the lowdown on the supply situation."

Tripper, his belly protruding over his belt, pulled himself from his chair and walked up to the head of the audience. "I'm gonna give you guys the bad news first. No individual weapons on this trip. We'll all carry M16s."

35

"For Chrissake!" Bullhorn Maywood boomed. "Why?"

"Because we're bringin' in weapons for the Pings," Tripper explained. "If we give 'em one kind o' rifle while we carry others, they'll think they're gettin' second best. It's the same ol' story the boys in the A detachments face."

"Big pain in ass!" Master Sergeant Kim said.

"Yeah, but there ain't nothin' we can do about it," Tripper said. "Naturally we'll be bringin' in supply bundles, so there's gotta be a detail to bring 'em in off—" He stopped and grinned as he remembered they'd be landing in abandoned rice paddies. "I mean bring 'em in *out* of the drop zone."

"Fun-ny!" Archie Dobbs said.

"What's funny is that you're on that detail," Tripper said. "Also Blue, Toby, Bullhorn, and me."

"What about resupply?" Calvin asked.

"There won't be any reg'larly scheduled drops on account o' we don't know for sure what we'll be doin', or when we'll be doin' it—or where either. So that phase o' the operation will be handled by the seat of our pants."

Top Gordon had a question. "Any special gear to take in with us?"

"Nope," the Tripper answered. "Again, this is because we don't know what's in store for us. If there ain't any more questions, I'll turn this over to Sparks for the commo part o' the briefback."

Sparks stayed at his seat, only standing up to deliver his short speech. "We'll be using Prick-Sixes for inter-detachment commo. The call signs will be Falcon for the command element, Alpha and Bravo for each team. We'll also have an AN/PRC-forty-one for the base camp. We'll be using a frequency of three twenty-five, and the call sign is Pingo."

Falconi motioned to him. "What about the crystals

for the Prick-Sixes?"

"I checked 'em out, skipper. All are the same."

"Good," the major said. "There's nothing worse than finding you can't contact the next team because of a difference in crystals."

Sparks nodded. "Malpractice will give you the medical portion of the briefback."

Malpractice McCorckel took the radioman's place. "We're gonna have to be cautious at first in our contacts with the Pings," he began. "I don't know their health status. They could have everything from the plague to leprosy. As soon as I check it out, I'll let you know. Same for their sanitary facilities, though a preliminary check shows they're pretty careful about latrines."

"What about VD?" Archie Dobbs asked.

Top Gordon interrupted. "It's already been established that we're to leave their women alone."

"Yeah? What if one of 'em won't leave *me* alone?"

"I'll place her under immediate psychiatric treatment," Malpractice said. "Now to continue. As always, use water purification tablets and be careful of insect bites and small abrasions or cuts. They can fester quickly out there. MEDEVAC is laid on from the base camp in case of casualties, and that will include the Pings." He looked over at Falconi. "That's it, skipper."

Falconi took the floor. "I've broken us down into teams again, and I'll post them so you know who'll go where. During the jump the Alphas have the left door, the Bravos the right. The command element will split up between them." He looked at Fagin and Andrea who had been sitting silently in the back of the room. "Anything to add to all this?"

Fagin stood up. "Nothing, except to say good luck."

Andrea smiled. "*Thurong-lo binh-an, bonne chance*," she said. "That is the same thing Chuck Fagin just said, except they are in the languages of my two bloodlines."

"I wish you was goin' with us, Andrea," Archie Dobbs said sincerely. "You done a damn good job on Operation Saigon Showdown."

"I wish I was, too," Andrea said. "And thank you for those kind words."

Falconi went to the wall and tacked a piece of paper to it. "These are the teams. Check them out, then let's get back to the isolation area. There's still lots of work to do."

The men, curious as to who they'd be working and fighting with, hurried to check out the roster:

COMMAND ELEMENT

Maj. Robert Falconi, commander
S.Sgt. Archie Dobbs, scout
PO2 Sparks Martin, radio operator
Sfc. Malpractice McCorckel, medic

ALPHA FIRE TEAM

M.Sgt. Top Gordon, team leader
Sfc. Calvin Culpepper, demo
S.Sgt. Bullhorn Maywood, rifleman
Sgt. Toby Barker, rifleman

BRAVO FIRE TEAM

M.Sgt. Chun Kim, team leader
PO3 Blue Richards, demo
Sfc. Ray Swift Elk, rifleman
S.Sgt. Charlie Tripper, rifleman

Each man quickly noted his assignment, then hurried from the briefback room back to Isolation.

CHAPTER THREE

Robert Mikhailovich Falconi was born an army brat at Fort Meade, Maryland in the year 1934.

His father, 2d Lt. Michael Falconi, was the son of Italian immigrants. The parents, Salvatore and Luciana Falconi, had wasted no time in instilling an appreciation of America and the opportunity offered by the nation into their youngest son as they had their other seven children. Mr. Falconi even went as far to name his son Michael rather than the Italian Michele. The boy had been born an American, was going to live as an American, so—*per Dio e tutti i santi*—he was going to be named as an American!

Young Michael was certainly no disappointment to his parents or older brothers and sisters. He studied hard in school and excelled. He worked in the family's small shoe repair shop in New York City's Little Italy during the evenings, doing his homework late at night. When he graduated from high school, Michael was eligible for several scholarships to continue his education in college, but even with this help, it would have entailed great sacrifice on the parts of his parents. Two older brothers, both working as lawyers, could have helped out a bit, but Michael didn't want to be any more of a burden on his family than was absolutely necessary.

He knew of an alternative. The nation's service academies, West Point and Annapolis, offered free education to qualified young men. Michael, through the local ward boss, received a congressional appointment to take the examinations to attend the United States Military Academy.

He was successful in this endeavor and was appointed to the Corps of Cadets. West Point didn't give a damn about his humble origins. It didn't matter to the Academy whether his parents were poor immigrants or not. West Point also considered the fact that his father, a struggling cobbler, had absolutely no meaning. All that institution was concerned about was whether Cadet Michael Falconi could cut it or not. It was this measuring of a man, by no other standards than his own abilities and talents, that caused the young plebe to develop a sincere, lifelong love for the United States Army. He finished his career at the school in the upper third of his class, sporting the three chevrons and rockers of a brigade adjutant on his sleeves upon graduation.

Second Lieutenant Falconi was assigned to the Third Infantry Regiment at Fort Meade, Maryland. This unit was a ceremonial outfit that provided details for military funerals at Arlington National Cemetery, the guard for the Tomb of the Unknown Soldier and other official functions in the Washington, D.C. area.

The young shavetail enjoyed the bachelor's life in the nation's capital, and his duties as protocol officer, though not too demanding, were interesting. He was required to be present during social occasions that were official affairs of state. He coordinated the affairs and saw to it that all the political bigwigs and other brass attending them had a good time. He was doing exactly those duties at such a function when he met a young

Russian Jewish refugee named Miriam Ananova Silberman.

She was a pretty brunette of twenty-years of age, who had the most striking eyes Michael Falconi had ever seen. He would always say all through his life that it was her eyes that captured his heart. When he met her, she was a member of the League of Jewish Refugees attending a congressional dinner. She and her father, Josef Silberman, had recently fled Joseph Stalin's anti-semitic terrorism in the Soviet Union. Her organization had been lobbying congress to enact legislation that would permit the American government to take action in saving European and Asian Jewry not only from the savagery of the Communists but also from the Nazis who had only begun their own program of intimidation and harassment of Germany's Jewish population.

When the lieutenant met the refugee beauty, he fell hopelessly in love. He spent that entire evening as close to her as he could possibly be while ignoring his other duties. He was absolutely determined he would get to know this beautiful Russian girl better. He begged her to dance with him at every opportunity, was solicitous about seeing to her refreshments, and engaged her in conversation, doing his best to be witty and interesting.

He was successful.

Miriam Silberman was fascinated by this tall, dark, and most handsome young officer. She was so swept off her feet that she failed to play any coquettish little games. His infectious smile and happy charm completely captivated the young woman.

The next day Michael began a serious courtship, determined to win her heart and marry the girl.

Josef Silberman was a cantankerous elderly widower. He opposed the match from the beginning. As a Talmud scholar, he wanted his only daughter to marry a nice

Jewish boy. But Miriam took pains to point out to him that this was America—a country that existed in direct opposition to any homogeneous customs. The mixing of nationalities and religions was not that unusual in this part of the world. Josef argued, stormed, forbade and demanded—but all for naught. In the end, so he would not lose the affections of his daughter, he gave his blessing. The couple was married in the post chapel at Fort Meade.

A year later their only child, a son, was born. He was named Robert Mikhailovich.

The boy spent his youth on various army posts. The only time he lived in a town or civilian neighborhood was during the three years his father, by then a colonel, served overseas in the European Theater of Operations in the First Infantry Division—the Big Red One. A family joke developed out of the colonel's service in that particular outfit. Robert would ask his dad, "How come you're serving in the First Division?"

The colonel always answered, "Because I figured if I was going to be one, I might as well be a Big Red One."

It was one of those private jokes that didn't go over too well outside the house.

The boy had a happy childhood. The only problem was his dislike of school. Too many genes of ancient Hebrew warriors and Roman legionnaires had been passed down to him. Robert was a kid who liked action, adventure, and plenty of it. The only serious studying he ever did was in the karate classes he took when the family was stationed in Japan. He was accepted in one of that island nation's most prestigious martial arts academies where he excelled while evolving into a serious and skillful *karateka*.

His use of this fighting technique caused one of the ironies in his life. In the early 1950s, his father had been posted as commandant of high school ROTC in San Diego, California. Robert, an indifferent student in that city's Hoover High School, had a run-in with some young Mexican-Americans. One of the Chicanos had never seen such devastation as that which Bobby Falconi dealt out with his hands. But he hung in there, took his lumps and finally went down from several lightning quick *shuto* chops that slapped consciousness from his enraged mind. A dozen years later, this same young gang member— named Manuel Rivera—once again met Robert Falconi. The former was a Special Forces sergeant first class and the latter a captain in the same elite outfit.

Sfc. Manuel Rivera, a Black Eagle, was killed in action during the raid on the prison camp in North Vietnam in 1964.

When Falconi graduated from high school in 1952, he immediately enlisted in the army. Although his father had wanted him to opt for West Point, the young man couldn't stand the thought of being stuck in any more classrooms. In fact, he didn't even want to be an officer. During his early days on army posts he had developed several friendships among career noncommissioned officers. He liked the attitudes of these rough-and-tumble professional soldiers who drank, brawled, and fornicated with wild abandon during their off-duty time. The sergeants' devil-may-care attitude seemed much more attractive to young Robert than the heavy responsibilities that seemed to make commissioned officers and their lives so serious and, at times, tedious.

After basic and advanced infantry training, he was shipped straight into the middle of the Korean war where he was assigned to the tough Second Infantry Division.

He participated in two campaigns there. These were designated by the United States Army as: Third Korean Winter and Korea Summer-Fall 1955. Robert Falconi

43

fought, roasted and froze in those turbulent months. His combat experience ranged from holding a hill during massive attacks by crazed Chinese Communist forces, to the deadly cat-and-mouse activities of night patrols in enemy territory.

He returned Stateside with a sergeancy, the Combat Infantryman's Badge, the Purple Heart, the Silver Star, and the undeniable knowledge that he had been born and bred for just one life—that of a soldier.

His martial ambitions also had expanded. He now desired a commission but didn't want to sink himself into the curriculum of the United States Military Academy. His attitude toward schoolbooks remained the same—to hell with 'em!

At the end of his hitch in 1955, he reenlisted and applied for Infantry Officers Candidate school at Fort Benning, Georgia.

Falconi's time in OCS registered another success in his life. He excelled in all phases of the rigorous course. He recognized the need for brain work in the classrooms and soaked up the lessons through long hours of study while burning the proverbial midnight oil in quarters. The field exercises were a piece of cake for this combat veteran, but he was surprised to find out that, even there, the instructors had plenty to teach him.

His only setback occurred during "Fuck-Your-Buddy-Week." That was a phase of the curriculum in which the candidates learned responsibility. Each man's conduct— or misconduct—was passed on to an individual designated as his buddy. If a cadet screwed up he wasn't punished. His buddy was. Thus, for the first time in many of these young men's lives, their personal conduct could bring joy or sorrow to others. Falconi's buddy was late to reveille one morning and he drew the demerit.

But this was the only setback in an otherwise spotless six months spent at OCS. He came out number one in his class and was offered a regular army commission. The brand new second lieutenant happily accepted the honor and set out to begin this new phase of his career in an army he had learned to love as much as his father did.

His graduation didn't result in an immediate assignment to an active duty unit. Falconi found himself once more in school—but these were not filled with hours over books. He attended jump school and earned the silver parachutist badge; next was ranger school where he won the coveted orange-and-black tab; then he was shipped down to Panama for jungle warfare school where he garnered yet one more insignia.

Following that he suffered another disappointment. Again, his desire to sink himself into a regular unit was thwarted. Because he held a regular army commission rather than a reserve one like his other classmates, Falconi was returned to Fort Benning to attend the Infantry School. The courses he took were designed to give him some thorough instruction in staff procedures. He came out on top here as well, but there was another thing that happened to him.

His intellectual side finally blossomed.

The theory of military science, rather than complete practical application, began to fascinate him. During his time in combat—and the later army schooling—he had begun to develop certain theories. With the exposure to Infantry School, he decided to do something about these ideas of his. He wrote several articles for the *Infantry Journal* about these thoughts—particularly on his personal analysis of the proper conduct of jungle and mountain operations involving insurgency and counterinsurgency forces.

The army was more than a little impressed with this lieutenant (he had been promoted) and sent him back to Panama to serve on a special committee that would develop and publish official U.S. Army policy on small unit combat in tropical conditions. He honed his skills and tactical expertise during this time.

From there he volunteered for Special Forces—The Green Berets—and was accepted. After completing the officers course at Fort Bragg, North Carolina, Falconi finally was assigned to a unit. This was the Fifth Special Forces Group in the growing conflict in South Vietnam.

Now a captain, he worked closely with ARVN units and even helped to organize village militias to protect hamlets against the Viet Cong and North Vietnamese. Gradually, his duties expanded until he organized and led several dangerous missions that involved deep penetration into territory controlled by the Communist guerrillas.

This activity brought him to the attention of a Central Intelligence Agency case officer named Clayton Andrews. Andrews had been doing his own bit of clandestine fighting which involved more than harassment in VC areas. His main job was the conduct of missions into North Vietnam itself. He arranged an interview with Captain Falconi to see if the officer would fit into his own sphere of activity. He found Falconi exactly the man he had been looking for. Pulling all the strings he had, Andrews saw to it that the Special Forces man was transferred to his own branch of SOG— the Special Operations Group—to begin work on a brand new project.

Captain Falconi was tasked with organizing a new fighting unit to be known as the Black Eagles. This group's basic policy was to be primitive and simple: Kill Or Be Killed!

Their mission was to penetrate deep into the heartland of the Communists to disrupt, destroy, maim, and slay. The men who would belong to the Black Eagles would be volunteers from every branch of the armed forces. And that was to include all nationalities involved in the struggle against the Red invasion of South Vietnam.

Each man was to be an absolute expert in his particular brand of military mayhem. He had to be an expert in not only his own nation's firearms but also those of other friendly and enemy countries. But the required knowledge in weaponry didn't stop at the modern ones. This also included knives, bludgeons, garrotes, and even crossbows when the need to deal silent death had arisen.

There was also a requirement for the more sophisticated and peaceful skills, too. Foreign languages, land navigation, communications, medical, and even mountaineering and scuba diving were to be within the realm of knowledge of the Black Eagles.

They became the enforcement arm of SOG, drawing the missions which were the most dangerous and sensitive. In essence they were hit men, closely coordinated and completely dedicated, held together and directed through the forceful personality of their leader, Maj. Robert Falconi.

As unit integrity and morale built up, the detachment decided they wanted an insignia all their own. This wasn't at all unusual for units in Vietnam. Local manufacturers, acting on decisions submitted to them by the troops involved, produced these emblems that were worn by the outfits while "in country." These adornments were strictly nonregulation and unauthorized for display outside of Vietnam.

Falconi's men came up with a unique beret badge manufactured as a cloth insignia. A larger version was used as a shoulder patch. The design consisted of a black eagle—naturally—with spread wings. Looking to its right, the big bird clutched a sword in one claw and a bolt of lightning in the other. Mounted on a khaki shield that was trimmed in black, the device was an accurate portrayal of its wearers: somber and deadly.

They even had an unofficial motto, though it wasn't

47

part of their insignia. The statement, in Latin, was simple and quite to the point:

CALCITRA CLUNIS

It translated as "kick ass."

CHAPTER FOUR

It was three-thirty in the morning as Major Falconi and Master Sergeant Gordon each inspected one of the C-123 aircraft's pair of doors to make sure no protruding objects or sharp edges were in evidence. Such obstructions, in the use of the static line-operated T10 parachutes, could spell disaster for a jumper. If the opening device was out, a complete malfunction would result.

Of course the unfortunate victim could always use the ripcord on his reserve parachute—but at a jump altitude of only eight hundred feet, he would have precious little time to get it deployed.

Top ran his hand along the edge of the door, working in the weak light that came from the large hangar nearby. "I think we oughta tape these up, skipper."

"Right," the Falcon replied. He pulled a roll of rigger tape from the large side pocket of his fatigues and tossed it over to the detachment sergeant. After fetching another for himself, he set to work applying several layers along the door where the static lines would be making contact.

The air was heavy and muggy, with the lights of Saigon still bright despite the fact it was so early in the morning.

It was almost ironic that these men about to embark on a trip straight into the hell of war, were within sight and sound of carefree revelry.

"That should take care of any potential problems with the static lines," Top said. "Now let's check the interior."

Falconi made sure the doors, removed for the jump, had been securely lashed to the deck of the aft cargo ramp. Both quickly inspected the seats to see that all were installed and locked in tight. While Top tested the red and green jump lights, the Falcon got on the intercom and ran a check with the pilot.

"Everything looks *kosher*—as they say in the Israeli paratroops," Top said.

"Right," Falconi said. "Let's chute up and have the personnel inspection." He looked at his watch. "We're running a couple of minutes late."

The two stepped down from the aircraft and joined the other Black Eagles who were busy arranging their personal gear and parachutes prior to donning them.

Top got the show on the road with just two words, "Chute up!"

There was an immediate bustle of activity as the men broke down into two-man buddy teams to struggle into the equipment. To an outsider, it would have looked like chaos, but the men's movements were quick and efficient, using habits born of countless operations both in war and in field training exercises back in the States.

Within moments they were ready for inspection. It may have seemed ridiculous for the Falcon and Top to personally see that each man had carefully put on his parachute, but a single moment of carelessness could prove fatal. Or, in the case of a twisted leg strap, quite painful when the offending strap of nylon locked down tight on somebody's scrotum. Archie Dobbs once did this and talked in a high soprano for two full hours after an uncomfortable descent.

"Let's go! Let's go!" Top barked. "After you're checked out, board the aircraft in reverse stick order."

When the last heavily laden man finally waddled awkwardly toward the boarding ladder, Falconi and Top took a couple of quick minutes to check each other out, then they joined the others.

The air force crew chief nodded to Falconi as the Black Eagles' commander climbed aboard. "How are you doing, sir?"

"Pretty good," Falconi answered. Then he recognized the man. "Aren't you Sergeant Padilla?"

"Yes, sir," the airman answered. "Been awhile since I've seen you guys."

"Sure has," Falconi said. "But I'll never forget it."

"Me neither," Padilla answered. "I remember hanging out the door of that C-forty-seven, watching you guys slowly disintegrate in that damned glider." He shook his head. "I'll tell you, sir, I didn't think you'd make it."

"Thanks to you and Colonel Baldwin we did, though," Falconi said.

The two were referring to the glider extraction the Black Eagles performed during their exfiltration from the mission area in the final, dangerous moments of Operation Laotian Nightmare.

"I noticed some new faces," Padilla remarked.

"Yeah, we've taken some casualties, so there's been a few replacements," Falconi said. "Say, what are you doing aboard this aircraft? I thought it belonged to the South Vietnamese."

"It does, sir, but there's an American copilot—and me—along as advisors. Since I know you personally, I thought I'd do more than just go along for the ride."

"I'm glad of that," Falconi said.

Padilla checked his watch. "Take off in five minutes, sir." He waved at the other members of the detachment.

51

"Good luck, you guys. It was nice seeing you again."

Archie Dobbs, up near the door, grinned at Padilla. "Don't take this personal, Steve, but ever'time we get mixed up with you, the shit seems to hit the fan."

Padilla grinned. "Think this'll be any different?"

"No way!" Archie said.

Padilla started to reply, but the engines kicked into life and the roar would have drowned out his words. So he gave the Black Eagles a silent thumbs-up signal and went forward to his position in the cockpit.

Within a couple of minutes, the large aircraft began slowly rolling to its takeoff position.

Lt.Col. Gregori Krashchenko couldn't sleep.

He stood in the open window of his hotel room and stared down at the empty streets of Hanoi as he chain-smoked the dry, fast-burning cigarettes of his native Soviet Union.

Krashchenko was in deep shit.

What made his situation so intolerable was that his first years of service to Mother Russia had been filled with glory, promotions, medals, and great promise. But if things kept going like they were now, instead of the epaulets of a general on his shoulders, he'd be struggling with bags of salt down in some Siberian mine.

Krashchenko was from the KGB, but he'd begun his military career in the Russian army after volunteering to serve in the elite units of the *parachotno-decantye*—the paratroops.

An eager student in school, he had carried his desire to please his superiors over into the army. As a junior lieutenant, his energetic bootlicking and toadyism quickly caught the attention of his regimental commissar.

What pleased this political officer so much was that

52

Krashchenko did more than display a great amount of attentiveness in the classes extolling the virtues of communism and socialism; he went a dozen or so steps further and wrote several treatises expounding the philosophies the commissar preached to the men.

This resulted in favorable reports sent forward praising the eager shavetail's qualities of loyalty. Eventually it was recommended that he be transferred from the role of line officer to the political branch of the Soviet army.

Krashchenko put the icing on the cake himself when he turned in a fellow officer who had been making unpatriotic remarks regarding the institutions of Communism and the Soviet government in general. Under normal circumstances, this action would have cinched the political officer's job, but Krashchenko was able to receive even a better advancement—and for a very good reason.

The man he turned in was his own cousin—the son of Krashchenko's favorite aunt.

This brought him to the attention of the KGB, and their probing investigation convinced this Committee of State Security that Lt. Gregori Krashchenko was their kind of guy. In a political system that could not survive or function without brigades of snitching finks and backstabbers, the lieutenant was a godsend to those in authority—even if they were atheists.

The KGB Academy proved another feather in his bonnet. He graduated with honors and was rewarded with an exciting assignment of counterinsurgency in the Ukraine. The local peasants, never too fond of their Russian masters, were fighting back in a manner that showed all evidence of soon getting completely out of hand. Krashchenko went after them and proved his deadly efficiency by bringing a detachment of East German police to massacre the dissident Ukrainians.

Since this was also considered on-the-job training for the Kraut Reds, it proved the fledgling KGB operative's efficiency without a doubt.

Krashchenko's career continued to soar as he turned his attention to other hardcases, and he pursued them straight into the hell of the Soviet concentration camp system without regard to their innocence or guilt.

Finally he received an assignment that was considered a plum. The North Vietnamese had sent disturbing reports to their Russian big brothers about a special detachment of raiders led by an American officer. This enigmatic group had been doing some real damage and immediate help was requested to handle them.

Krashchenko, now a lieutenant colonel, was sent to Hanoi where he teamed up with Maj. Truong Van of the North Vietnamese army, G2. This major, an order-of-battle expert, was among the first to properly identify the raiders, so he was assigned to Krashchenko as an assistant and interpreter.

Within months, utilizing a North Vietnam agent named Xong and his Saigon organization, they had managed to blackmail a South Vietnamese colonel named Ngai Quang into ferreting out information on this detachment of the Americans' Special Operations Group. Thus, within a very short time, Krashchenko knew all about Major Falconi and his Black Eagles.

And part of this involved a very curious point in Soviet law.

Falconi's mother, it was learned, was a Jewish refugee who had illegally fled the Soviet Union in the early 1930s. By Russian statutes, she was still a citizen of the Workers' and Peasants' Paradise, and that meant her son Robert Mikhailovich also belonged to Russia—whether he wanted to or not.

Thus, if Falconi could be captured, it would be lawfully proper (under the Communist system) to take him back to the Soviet Union to be tried as both a traitor and a war criminal. Then he could be shot or used as a propaganda ploy to embarrass the West.

All that was necessary was to get their hands on him.

But, alas for poor Krashchenko, from that point on, all his plans, aims, and operations had gone completely, wholly and undeniably to hell. Not only did his efforts not produce the desired results, they caused the destruction of a North Vietnamese infantry battalion, the end of a planned nuclear reactor in Laos, the loss of an elite detachment of East German police—not to mention the capture of their leader, the obliteration of Xong's intelligence net in Saigon, and a complete disruption of operations along the Ho Chi Minh Trail.

Krashchenko's aide, Major Truong, had also turned nasty. He had once been respectful and polite toward him. But with this mountain of failures, the North Vietnamese officer now openly sneered at the Russian, insulting him and even laughing at his efforts.

Now Krashchenko took a final drag off the bitter cigarette, then flipped the remnants down onto the street three stories below. He was playing his final card now, and if it was trumped, he might as well take that Tokarev pistol he kept in his suitcase and blow his Slavic brains out.

His whole plan hinged on a specially recruited battalion of Viet Cong. Krashchenko had harangued, begged, threatened, and bellowed until he had gotten this elite unit organized and superbly equipped. Now they waited down below the border of South Vietnam. At the first word of Black Eagle activity—no matter where it was—this battalion, complete with waiting helicopters, would be rushed to the operational area. The Black Eagles would find themselves facing a unit as dedicated and elite as themselves.

Krashchenko lit another cigarette, then spoke aloud,

"I am thinking of you, Major Falconi. You are even in my dreams, you gangster! Your days of glory will descend as mine rise once again. Soon, Robert Mikhailovich Falconi, you will be going up against *partisan ot adski*— guerrillas from hell!"

The Black Eagles, their static line snap fasteners locked over the twin anchor cables that ran the length of the fuselage, pressed tightly together. All men had their eyes on the red glow of the jump lights. As soon as the green bulbs lit up, they knew they would rush toward the door to hurl themselves out into the brightening crimson sky of dawn.

Chief Master Sergeant Padilla, standing by the door, leaned close to Falconi's ear. "Good luck, sir."

Falconi nodded his thanks—then the green light flashed on.

He leaped through the door into the roaring push of the prop blast. Falconi could feel the deployment bag pull away from his backpack and could sense the suspension lines zipping out of their stowage loops.

The big canopy of the T10 blossomed into life, and his fall was braked. Top certainly hadn't been lying about the drop zone. It was a series of rice paddies—wet ones—that stretched out below him in the faint light. The water was supposed to be relatively shallow, so the Falcon decided to make a regular parachute landing fall—or get as close to one as possible—rather than jettisoning his chute in a water landing.

He stared down at his boots, watching the water under them come up closer—closer—closer—then he perceived a splash and he went into the cool wetness. Blind instinct got him to his feet, and he turned, muddy and dripping to watch the rest of the detachment come splashing into the operational area.

56

Off to one side, he perceived several small Oriental men running toward him. Falconi quickly dropped his gear and retrieved the M16 rifle, stripping the protective covering from the weapon. The approaching party, all smiles, waved at him. As soon as they drew closer, one said, "You come to play ping-pong?"

Falconi recognized the challenge, and he answered it properly. "No, we've come to play other games."

The spokesman's grin widened. "Ah! You are Falconi?"

"Yes. And you?"

"I am Tsang *Shiu-Wai*—Captain Tsang. I am leader of Ping-Yan-Uen."

Falconi offered his hand. "Glad to know you."

"Me too, oh-you-kid! Ha! Ha!" Tsang said. "Come with me. We fight now."

"Fight?" Falconi asked puzzled. "Now?"

"Ah, yes! I send men to get Viet Cong to chase them," Tsang explained. "They lead them here. We have nice fight. Okay?"

"Christ!" Falconi said. "Doesn't sound like I have much of a choice."

Falconi heard some splashing behind him and turned to see Top Gordon leading the rest of the detachment. The major waved at him. "Get those weapons ready. VC in the vicinity."

"Damn it!" Top swore. "How'd they get here?"

"I'll explain the Ping's idea of drop-zone security later," Falconi said. "But you're not going to believe me."

A few quick hand signals was all that was necessary to form the Black Eagles into their fire teams. With Tsang and the Pings leading the way, Falconi's men formed up as skirmishers and advanced cautiously out of the rice paddies toward the jungle.

Within the space of only a minute, firing broke out

57

ahead of them. Tsang, the Ping leader, yelled out an order in Chinese, and his men charged forward.

Falconi, though leery as hell, knew the impressions formed on this first encounter were all important. He had to damn his misgivings and order the detachment to join the attack.

Spurts of water exploded as rounds splashed around them. Top Gordon, a few paces behind his Alpha Fire Team, ordered them to spread out a bit more. "And keep alert! We don't even know where the Charlies are."

The question was quickly answered, however, by the sudden explosion of automatic weapons fire to their front. One of the Pings, fifteen yards ahead, suddenly jerked as several bullets stitched his torso. He went down in a heap as his buddies leaped over him and pressed on. Two more of them fell before the Alpha Fire Team cut loose into the target area with their M16s.

This disciplined fire accomplished two things: It forced the Viet Cong gunners to duck and be more cautious, and it also brought a bit of order to the chaos of the undirected battle. The Pings, noticing the Black Eagles maintaining both combat formations and well-aimed firing, pulled away to watch this form of fighting they were not familiar with.

Falconi flipped on his Prick-Six radio. "This is Falcon," he said into the mouthpiece. "Commo check. Over."

Top Gordon's voice came in loud and clear. "This is Alpha. Over."

"This is Bravo. Over," said Chun Kim in his Korean accent.

"This is Falcon. The target area is between the edge of the farthest paddy and that bamboo grove over there. Spread out and lay down a base of fire and maintain it 'til you hear from me again. Over."

"Wilco. Out," Top replied.

"Okay. Out," Kim said.

Falconi turned to the command element. Everyone was ready to move out on his order. Sparks Martin had dropped off the big radio. Like the others he was lean and mean, ready to fight.

"Listen up," the Falcon said. "This situation is a cluster-fuck, but we can take advantage of it. Charlie's got no back up and probably doesn't know for sure what's going on. He's undoubtedly used to these hit-and-run affairs with the Pings and doesn't expect anything special."

Archie Dobbs, anxious to get into the fray, nodded excitedly. "That means we can get behind 'em without much trouble, right, skipper?"

"Right," Falconi said. "It'll be simple and fast. The Alphas and Bravos can keep 'em pinned down until we circle 'em. A couple of grenades each should do the trick."

"We go, too!" Tsang said. He had been squatting nearby, waiting to see how Falconi would fight the battle.

"Fine," Falconi said. But he added diplomatically, "But we'll do the work, okay? My men are out of practice."

It made sense to Tsang. "Okay, oh-you-kid!"

Falconi motioned to Archie, Sparks, and Malpractice, leading them into the jungle. After they had penetrated the heavy vegetation for twenty meters, they turned inward, working their way back toward the sound of the firing.

It took a hard fifteen minutes of travel before they reached a point directly behind the Viet Cong. Using only hand-and-arm signals, Falconi spread out his small group, and they advanced cautiously toward the enemy. When he reached a position he considered favorable, the Black Eagle commander spoke softly into the radio. "This is Falconi. Cease fire. Out."

The volume of shooting immediately dropped as the Alphas and Bravos followed the orders to avoid hitting any of the men in the command element.

Archie Dobbs, easing ahead of the group by habit, was the first to make contact. He spotted a VC clad in the black pajama uniform of his "army." The Charlie, facing the opposite direction, had leaves stuck in a band around his head. He methodically squeezed off fire bursts with a Chinese type 56 light machine gun.

Archie, peering from behind a tree, sat his rifle down and eased a grenade off his harness. He just started to toss the device when he caught a movement in the corner of his eye. He turned and found himself facing a very surprised young VC. The kid must have been fifteen or sixteen years old. But he was still dangerous.

Archie displayed his most charming smile. "Catch!" he said. He flipped the grenade at the Red and ducked behind a tree.

The insurgent, inexperienced and stunned, did as he had been requested. He grabbed the grenade in both hands, holding onto it for one stupid second. Then he realized what he was doing and threw it away in a panic. Unfortunately for the machine gunner, it flopped down next to him. He only had time for a quick glance before it went off, shredding the flesh off his upper body and throwing him and his weapon over into the denser vegetation.

Archie, his M16 leveled, sprung from behind the tree and fired a burst into the youth. The Viet Cong staggered back and went down in a tangle of arms and legs. The American shook his head. "Damn, fellah! This just wasn't your day, was it?" He glanced at the mutilated gunner. "Or yours either, huh?"

Off to both sides of Archie, the rest of the command element had taken care of their individual targets. The success of the small operation was punctuated by grenades and the short barks of the M16s. Falconi, standing over the shrapnel-torn body of a Red rifleman, once again spoke into his radio. "This is Falcon. Situation under control. Move in. Out."

The Ping captain, Tsang, came out of the bushes. "Hey! You make nice fight. Nobody killed of you fellahs, huh?"

Falconi shook his head. "Nope."

"Two of my men now general," Tsang said.

"We'll have to talk about keeping the others enlisted men for a longer period of time," Falconi said. "I think soldiers are more important than generals right now."

"Sometimes, yes!" Tsang agreed. "We talk about it."

The Alphas and Bravos moved through the trees and linked up with the command element. Top and Kim arranged their men in an impromptu defensive perimeter and let them sit down.

Tsang observed the activity with a wide grin. "Hey! Good idea! After fight we too happy to expect more trouble."

"That can be dangerous," Falconi said.

Tsang laughed aloud. "Oh, yes! But no matter. Ever'body want to be general anyhow!"

Falconi and Top Gordon gave each other a foreboding look. The master sergeant licked his dry lips. "I think this operation is going to be a hell of a lot hairier than we expected."

Falconi, saying nothing, felt a feeling close to dread. He turned to Tsang. "Well, shall we gather our supplies out of the rice paddies and get to base camp?"

"Sure thing!" Tsang said happily. "Fun just start, oh-you-kid!"

CHAPTER FIVE

The afternoon heat pressed down on the jungle trail like a steamy, invisible cloud. The high temperature seemed to boil the moisture out of the soil. Thousands of insects buzzed in this environment they found so comfortable and exhilarating as they flitted from leaf to leaf, flower to flower—and man to man.

The Black Eagles, soaked in perspiration that offered no cooling effect because of the inability for it to evaporate, endured this natural hell in unmoving silence.

The only sound, besides the insidious bugs, was the gentle hissing of the Prick-Six radios that had been turned on and kept close to each team leader's ear. There would be no speaking into the sets for communication, only the careful pushing of the transmit buttons to break the whisper of dead air.

This was the best way to communicate on an ambush site.

Falconi licked at the sweat on his upper lip. Tsang, the Ping captain, squatted beside him, his face impassive despite the discomfort. Archie Dobbs, only a couple of meters away, yet completely invisible, kept a sharp eye on the trail. On the other side, both Malpractice and Sparks manned their positions in silent alertness. They were situated at the head of the ambush. As the front security force, they would close in that end of the assault when the attack force cut loose on the targets.

Down on the other end was the rear security force, who were tasked with sewing up things in their portion of the operation. This was Chun Kim's Bravo Team made up of Blue Richards, Ray Switt Elk, and the Tripper. All were poised and ready when the ambush went down.

Top Gordon's Alphas, augmented with a dozen Pings, were the attack force. Depending on the code that Archie Dobbs sent over the small radio, Top would launch the assault on the unwary VC that were supposed to be using the trail sometime that afternoon.

The insects, now encouraged by the Black Eagles' lack of resistance to their efforts, became bolder as they landed on bare skin and stuck stingers into the tempting flesh. Each man, not daring to make a sound, gritted his teeth and cursed bugdom in unspoken blasphemies that would have turned the air blue if they could have been heard.

Archie Dobbs, the point man as usual, suddenly came alert. He'd heard a sharp noise. It might have been a Viet Cong stepping on a dead twig, or merely the clack of some small jungle animal. He waited a few moments more and heard the faint rustling of brush as if men were passing through leafy branches while walking through the rain forest.

Finally, Archie caught sight of the bare feet encased in sandals as they passed his position on the trail. He reached out and pressed the Prick-Six's button three times.

Up and down the ambush site, all thoughts of physical discomfort disappeared. The adrenaline flowed now, and the men's senses leaped to full wakefulness.

Archie waited until he was sure the final man had passed, then he hit the button again.

Down in the attack force, Top Gordon had timed the seconds between each of Archie's signals. It had taken approximately fifteen seconds. Top estimated there were twelve VC in the column. His M16, already charged with the safety off, was ready to go as he peered through the brush until a dozen of the Reds had passed his point of observation.

The twelfth man caught a fireburst of three rounds into the side. Blood splattered from the wound and poured out the Viet Cong's nose and mouth as he danced sideways under the impact of the slugs. He fell in an undignified heap on the other side of the trail.

At almost the same moment Top fired, the others of the attack force sprayed bullets from their weapons into their zones of fire.

It didn't take long.

Within moments, the jungle was silent. Even the insects, startled by the sudden explosive violence around them, had buzzed upward in an instinctive, frantic effort to get away from the cordite smell and concussion that had ruined their pleasant afternoon.

Down on the trail, sprawled on the hot, damp ground, were the bodies of a dozen Viet Cong. Some, with their pajama uniforms soaked in blood, appeared as if they were sleeping calmly, while others stared sightlessly up at the men who had just blown their lives away. There were also a couple whose features had been blasted into pulpy masses.

The smell of warm blood overcame the insects' natural fear. They came swarming back down to this fresh meat, buzzing in frantic obscenity as they drank the exposed blood.

Archie Dobbs, leading the front security force to the main ambush site, arrived. He looked down at the cadavers and the swarming bugs. "Little motherfuckers," he said to himself.

"Who?" Malpractice behind him wanted to know. "The Viet Cong or them insects?"

"Both," Archie spat.

Maj. Truong Van, seated at his desk, lit a cigarette. He dropped the match in an ashtray and slowly exhaled a cloud of smoke. He looked insolently over at the figure of Lieutenant Colonel Krashchenko as the Russian stared grimly out the window of the office they shared.

Truong had plenty of responsibility in the North Vietnamese army. A senior intelligence officer and order-of-battle specialist, his principle duties had been to keep track of American units and their key officers during the rapid buildup in the south. He'd been abruptly pulled from those duties several months previously and assigned to work with Krashchenko.

At first Truong had been extremely respectful of the Soviet officer. The man, being from the much feared KGB, was reputed to be an absolute machine of efficiency. Truong had deferred to him repeatedly, speaking most humbly and maintaining a low profile as the Russian conducted his campaign to destroy the American gangster Falconi and the Black Eagles.

But, as time went on, this diety out of Moscow began more and more to show that he had feet of clay. One big mistake and defeat after the other were piled on top of misdirections and misconceptions, until Krashchenko's campaign had disintegrated into a mess. To make things worse, the Russian's concept of Orientals and their psychology was unrealistic and in grave error. But, because of his limited intellect, he was unable to change his perception of Indochinese people. In fact, like most Russians, Gregori Krashchenko was an out-and-out racist.

Truong took another drag off his cigarette. "You seem

to spend most of your time staring out of windows. A ruble for your thoughts, comrade."

Krashchenko, who was very much aware of Truong's feelings toward him, turned and sneered. "And a piaster for yours."

"My thoughts are not worth a piaster," Truong said smiling.

Krashchenko chortled. "I'm not surprised."

"They are not worth that, because I was thinking of your efforts against Falconi."

Krashchenko's face clouded over with anger. "You will regret those words. And all the other disrespect you have shown me over these past months."

Truong stared at his cigarette. "I think I shall regret them as much as Falconi regrets having you chase after him, comrade."

Rage welled up in Krashchenko. "I am a Soviet officer! A member of the KGB! I will not tolerate insubordination from a slant-eyed weasel!" He gasped, swallowing as his shouting took away his breath. Finally, after a few moments, he was able to speak again, though only in an angry whisper. "I shall report you, Truong."

"Fine," Truong said. He reached over and pushed his telephone toward the Russian. "The correct department to turn me in is the Special Security Bureau. Simply ask for the number four-two when the operator comes on the line."

Krashchenko clinched his teeth in anger. "You are going to be shot—shot—*shot*!"

Truong laughed aloud. "Then I shall undoubtedly die—die—*die*!"

"You little bastard monkey!" Krashchenko hissed. "You're going to be the sorriest man in Southeast Asia before another month has gone by."

"I am already sorrier than Major Falconi," Truong said. "I feel safe in assuming that he is the *happiest* man in Southeast Asia."

"You are insulting your own countrymen if you lack faith in this operation," Krashchenko said.

"On the contrary, comrade, I have every bit of faith in my countrymen," Truong said. "And the basic plan, too. Having a battalion of elite guerrillas standing by is excellent. Especially when they are under the command of Maj. Dnang Quong. He has been fighting the foreign invaders of Indochina since he was a young recruit in the Viet Minh. Each and every man in his battalion is handpicked and tested. Not only for political reliability but for soldiering skill and physical hardiness, too. I believe I can safely assume they are going to prove to be the force that can eventually destroy Falconi and his Black Eagles. They can accomplish that end, provided—"

"Provided what?" Krashchenko demanded.

"That you keep your fat Russian nose out of it, you afterbirth of a Cossack gang rape!"

"I'll kill you!" Krashchenko bellowed.

Truong quickly slipped a Chinese model 51 automatic pistol from his khaki tunic's interior. He aimed the weapon dead on Krashchenko's face. "I think not, comrade."

"You dare to point a pistol at a KGB officer!"

Truong playfully let the muzzle roam between his Russian companion's head and belt buckle. "The only problem I am having is choosing where to put the bullet."

Krashchenko, despite his rage, recognized the danger-ous situation he was in. Without being in good favor with the powers that be, he could be shot and dumped in a drainage ditch without the slightest concern of his KGB superiors. They would simply dispatch another officer to take his place.

The Russian glared at the North Vietnamese for several seconds, then turned and went back to staring out the window. Although, Truong didn't realize it, Krashchenko had already decided to allow Major Quong to command his battalion without outside direction. It had dawned on him that the complexity and scope of the situation warranted giving such a skilled insurgency commander a completely free hand.

This has been my error in the past, his mind told him. *I have tried to put in too much personal direction.* This time, with a *South* Vietnamese Viet Cong commander operating in his home area, success was practically guaranteed. But the Russian was still nervous and anxious.

Krashchenko looked at Truong's reflection in the window. *And you, you little yellow asshole*, his mind said silently, *will be singing another tune in front of the firing squad. Both you and that bastard Falconi!*

Falconi cradled the bowl of fish and rice in his left hand, and used his right to manipulate the chop sticks as he fed himself. The Ping-Yan-Uen leader Tsang, noisily gulping down his own supper, sat beside him. The two were the only ones at a table located toward the front of the eating hut. The lesser ranking Black Eagles and Ping soldiers gave close attention to their own meals at other tables.

This was the special hut in which the soldiers ate. The women and children had their own dining area. It was quite an important thing in a boy's life when took his first meal with the men. It was a time of celebration and pride for his father and older male relatives. This was the first significant event after the indoctrination and ceremonial acceptance as a Ping-Yan-Uen soldier.

Falconi sat his bowl down and treated himself to a drink of strong green tea. He looked at Tsang. "You have not commented on the ambush."

Tsang stopped eating. "Very interesting, oh-you-kid."

Falconi frowned in puzzlement. "Where did you pick up that 'oh-you-kid' thing?"

"From my grandfather," Tsang explained. "He was with the Americans during the Seige of Peking. They all the time say to Chinese girl, 'I love my wife but oh-you-kid.' So, when he teach me English, he tell me that what Americans allatime say to each other."

Falconi grinned. "It's a bit outdated, but it'll do."

"Twenty-three skidoo," Tsang said. "What you think I am—a rube?"

"Not me!" Falconi said laughing. "But let's get back to the ambush. What is your judgement?"

"I think it very nice—quick," Tsang said.

"Yes. It was quick," Falconi answered. "But there was something else about it."

"What?"

"None of our guys got killed."

Tsang shrugged. "Okay."

"That doesn't seem to mean much to you."

"A man want to die in battle sometime. Maybe later than sooner, but allasame want to die in battle," Tsang said.

"I'm aware of your beliefs," Falconi said. "But we don't want too many men to die, understand? If too many die, then we won't be able to fight anymore."

"Sure. That true. But that never happen. We got generals to help us," Tsang argued. "We pray to them for to tell us what to do."

"But if the generals are mad at you, they make you lose men, don't they?"

"Sure, oh-you-kid. But they not let us lose everyone. They let some live for when Chin-Sza-Tung come," Tsang explained.

"Chin-Sza-Tung? Who the hell is that?"

"She is Warrior-Sister. She will come to the Ping-Yan-Uen from the sky when the time is right," Tsang said matter-of-factly. "Then we conquer all of China and the *shiu-wai*—that me—will be emperor."

"Wait a minute," Falconi said. Evidently Chuck Fagin's lecture on the Ping's religion wasn't complete. "A woman soldier is going to lead you to your ultimate victory?"

"You bet, oh-you-kid! Like I tell you. Her name is Chin-Sza-Tung the Warrior-Sister. She will come to us from the sky someday, and we do like she say. Then we rule over all of China."

Falconi was thoughtful for several moments. "Very interesting, Tsang. Yes, indeed!"

Tsang nodded. "Yes. She take us to our glory. Warrior-Sister very beautiful woman, too. But nobody can make fuck with her."

"Well," Falconi said, "you can't have everything. I mean, you can't have somebody come along and help you conquer the world and give you a piece of ass, too."

"Sure," Tsang said. "I not greedy." He went back to eating.

Falconi got to his feet. "I have some business to attend to, Tsang. I'll see you later."

"Okay, oh-you-kid."

Falconi walked past the table where Sparks Martin was sitting. He signaled to the radio operator. "Let's get over to the AN/PRC-forty-one. There's a message I want to transmit back to Fagin."

"Aye, aye, sir," the sailor said, quickly getting to his feet.

Maj. Dnang Quong studied the map of Indochina with his good right eye. The left was covered by a black patch. There were several large marks on the topographical document. Each gave the location of a Black Eagles' operation and the dates it took place.

The Viet Cong officer had been trying to see if there was a pattern to Major Falconi's forays into war, but there was none. Obviously, the Black Eagles operated wherever opportunities or necessities in the tactical situation dictated.

Dnang had been contemplating the map and the intelligence he'd been given through the Russian Krashchenko for the past several weeks. He had hoped to determine where the next attack by the Black Eagles would take place. Then he would know where he'd be taking his elite battalion of Viet Cong.

His thoughts were interrupted by the arrival of his adjutant Lieutenant Trun. Trun, a young idealist completely dedicated to Communism and its insurgency in the south, stepped into the thatched hut that served as the battalion's headquarters. He noted his commander's activities. "Have you figured out anything yet, comrade major?"

Dnang shook his head. "No. There is no way to forecast the next mission of the gangsters." Dnang was a rugged-looking man. Compact and muscular, there wasn't an ounce of fat on his body. As a physical fitness fanatic, he submitted himself to martial arts exercises as well as the normal demands of guerrilla warfare.

The loss of his eye had occurred during a three-day interrogation he had endured by French paratroopers in 1953. He'd been a young platoon leader then, captured during an attack on an isolated outpost. When his Viet Minh unit renewed their assault, they finally captured the place and found him unconscious and close to death. It had been obvious he hadn't talked despite a hard interrogation.

Trun also studied the map for awhile. "I am pleased we have been entrusted with the destruction of the Black Eagles, but the thought has occurred to me that we won't have been the first elite unit to go against them."

"That is true," Dnang said. "The concept of sending specially formed units after the Black Eagles has been tried before. The concept, while good, failed because of a certain amount of oversight. We, on the other hand, are special in our knowledge of the terrain and country where we shall meet them."

Trun was puzzled. "But weren't the Laotian comrades who fought them about the nuclear reactor operating in their own home territory?"

"Yes, comrade," Dnang answered. "But I fear the Pathet Lao have a tendency to become over excited. They made unwise moves that cost them dearly in casualties."

"And the Three hundred twenty-seventh Infantry of the North Vietnam army?" Trun inquired. "They were defeated on the Song Bo River."

"Again—unfortunate tactical decisions."

Trun nodded in agreement. "What is your opinion of the efforts of the East Germans? They were completely destroyed, and their commander was captured."

"Yes—but remember he was part of an exchange the East European comrade made, so that was not a total loss," Dnang said. "As for the conduct of their operations—well, they were not used to jungle fighting. And they were far from home without an adequate logistical service available to them."

"Which will most certainly not be our problem."

"Of course not," Dnang said. "We have support among the peasants, even if they don't want to give it to us. And there's hardly a square meter of ground in either North *or* South Vietnam over which I have not fought."

"Yes!" Trun replied with enthusiasm. "And if the local populace cannot aid us, we have been promised unlimited supplies of the best quality from the North Vietnamese quartermaster department."

"The only difficulty we must face now is controlling our impatience," Dnang said. "But, sooner or later, the

73

Black Eagles will surface. And when they do, we shall move in on them."

They were interrupted by the distant sound of singing men. The voices grew steadily louder as the group drew closer. "That will be the battalion back from training," Trun said.

"I shall take the comrade soldiers' salutes," Dnang said. He left the map table and walked to the open porch of the hut. He had only to wait a few minutes before the first rank of his men appeared out of the jungle as they marched into the open area of the encampment. The hamlet boomed with the "International" as the Viet Cong guerrillas marched in perfect step.

Dnang stood at attention and saluted sharply. The pride he felt was strong and sure as he watched these handpicked veterans parade by. Every man in a leadership position—from company commander down to squad leader—was a battle-proven veteran of the old Viet Minh who had fought long and hard against the French. The soldiers themselves had also seen combat, though not in the old days, and were young, fit, enthusiastic, and full of optimism.

Dnang watched them continue on to their cantonment area. He turned to his young adjutant. "The men are primed for the coming fight."

Trun nodded enthusiastically. "Yes, comrade major! The American gangsters are unaware of the power that is about to be unleashed against them."

Dnang laughed. "They will be aware of the imminent defeat within five minutes of the first battle!"

Chuck Fagin, seated at his desk, took a final sip of the cold coffee and sat the cup down. He lit a cigarette, then leaned back in the straight-back chair and blew the smoke toward the ceiling.

74

It was a bit past midnight, and he was near exhaustion. There had been a change in the overall operational plans involving the Black Eagles, and he had been forced to put in some late hours revising contingencies involving supplies and munitions. It was all routine, but it had to be done in order to insure a smooth running mission.

Now, with the finished paperwork stacked neatly in front of him, he could at last relax and let his concern drain away. Fagin got to his feet and went over to the wet bar in the corner of the office. He made himself an Irish whiskey on the rocks and took a deep, long, and satisfying drink.

The intercom buzzer on the wall sounded. He reached over and hit the talk button. "Yeah?"

"Big Ben has struck—" came the code words.

"Twelve oh five," Fagin said, completing the phrase. "What's up?"

"Message, Mr. Fagin."

"Right." He walked out to the outer room and opened the door. An MP guard handed him an envelope. Fagin took it and went back inside to his desk. It was a message from Ping—the Black Eagle call sign for the present operation.

Fagin treated himself to another swig of whiskey, then sat down to read the rather lengthy missive. When he finished, the CIA officer smiled to himself and spoke aloud:

"Well, this should be real exciting for Andrea Thuy."

Then he finished his drink and immediately went back to the bar for another.

CHAPTER SIX

Andrea Thuy was so curious she could hardly contain herself. But the Oriental side of her personality helped her maintain a placid expression on her beautiful face. "Why all these questions, Chuck?"

Chuck Fagin, looking at her from behind his desk, held up his hand in a calming gesture. "Just continue to answer these, please," he said. "Now. You've had HALO experience, right?"

"High Altitude Low Opening free-fall parachute jumps? Of course," Andrea said.

"And how's your Cantonese?"

"Fluent," she replied. "When I lack much opportunity to speak it, I always read as much as I can besides listening to special broadcasts in that dialect from Radio Red China." A thought suddenly occurred to her, and she leaned forward, putting her hands on top of the desk. "You're thinking of committing me to an operation, aren't you?"

"Yes," Fagin admitted.

"Where? When?"

"Just a minute, young lady, I have one more question to ask you."

Andrea stood back. "Go ahead."

"It's a serious one—a *very* serious one—and I want a straight answer," Fagin said.

"Sure."

"I'm not fooling around, Andrea. I want you to—"

"Damn it, Chuck! Ask the goddamned question!"

"Okay." He paused. "Are you still in love with Robert Falconi?"

"Damn it! You'll never let me forget that, will you?" Andrea said under her breath. She knew that falling in love with the Black Eagles' commander had not been a smart thing to do. But a woman—even one who is a dedicated agent against Communism—is forever fighting with her emotions. Her romance with Falconi had been the result of losing just such a battle with her heart.

She would never forget that one and only time she'd let her defenses down and became a woman in love.

It had started out as a simple date for some dinner and dancing. It seemed like a normal thing to do. After all, they had been working closely together in the formulation and preparation for Operation Hanoi Hellground. She'd accepted Falconi's request to go on the town with him out of a desire to know him better and, she had to admit, because of a growing attraction for the American officer. She had experienced sexual activity with men before, but always in the line of duty. Andrea Thuy had never really made love with someone she cared about.

They'd headed for their evening of diversion dressed as civilians with the expressed desire to forget the war for awhile and simply enjoy themselves. The date evolved through a quiet dinner to some dancing and finally—a small room in a back-street hotel where she'd succumbed happily to his lovemaking.

Their *liaison d'amour* was interrupted by a phone call. Falconi had cursed the order to always let MACV-SOG aware of his exact location. The lovers had to hurriedly dress to return to Peterson Field to go into the isolation phase of what was to become the Black Eagles' first mission.

Falconi and Andrea managed to keep their coupling a secret between themselves until their return from the mission. But their solicitous caring and affection for each other became apparent to everyone concerned.

Clayton Andrews, when he was promoted upward from the Black Eagles' CIA case officer and replaced by Chuck Fagin, had informed the new man of the relationship between the detachment commander and the beautiful Andrea Thuy.

Fagin had made a quick and logical decision. A love affair involving operatives was the absolute worse thing that could happen between them. He'd immediately pulled Andrea off active ops and put her into a paperwork position in his office.

Now, with more than a year elapsed since the affair, Andrea stood looking at Chuck Fagin. "You're thinking about sending me in with the Black Eagles, aren't you?"

"Yes," Fagin said. "And in a most unusual role."

"Then let me tell you something, Chuck," Andrea said. "I am over any romantic involvement with Robert. You may, or may not, be aware of it, but he and I had a final discussion. We decided we weren't in love. I think I proved that in Operation Saigon Showdown."

"Yes, I suppose you did," Fagin said. He remembered how she'd gone fully and completely committed into the role of an expensive call girl, giving herself to any man who had the price. He looked straight into her face. "All right, Andrea. You're going out into the cold. And in the most unusual role you'll ever play in your entire life."

"Really? What am I to be?"

Fagin smiled. "My dear, you are to be nothing less than a goddess!"

*　　*　　*

79

Andrea Thuy, a first lieutenant in the South Vietnamese army, was a beautiful Eurasian woman in her mid-twenties. Five feet, six inches tall, she was svelte and trim, yet had large breasts and shapely hips and thighs that rounded out even her uniforms with a provocative shape.

Andrea was born in a village west of Hanoi in the late 1940s. Her father, Dr. Gaston Roget, was a lay missionary physician of the Catholic church. Deeply devoted to his native patients, the man served a large area of northern French Indochina in a dedicated, unselfish manner. The man did not stint a bit in the giving of himself and his professional talents.

He met Andrea's mother just after the young Vietnamese woman had completed her nurse's training in Hanoi. Despite the difference in their races and ages—the doctor by then was forty-eight years old—the two fell in love and were married. This blending of East and West produced a most beautiful child, young Andrea Roget.

Andrea's life was one of happiness. The village where she lived was devoted to *Bac-si* Gaston, as they called her father, and this respect was passed on to the man's wife and child. When the first hint of a Communist uprising brushed across the land, the good people of this hamlet rejected it out of hand. The propaganda the Reds vomited out did not fit when applied to the case of the gentle French doctor who devoted his time to looking after them.

The fanatical Communist movement could not ignore this open repudiation of their ideals. Therefore, the local Red guerrilla unit made a call on the people who would not follow the line of political philosophy they taught. To make the matter even more insidious, these agents of Soviet imperialism had hidden the true aims of their organization within the wrappings of a so-called independence movement. Many freedom-loving Indochinese

80

fervently wanted the French out of their country so they could enjoy the fruits of self-government. They were among the first to fall for the trickery of the Communist revolution.

When the Red Viet Minh came to the village, they had no intentions of devoting the visit to pacification or even winning the hearts and minds of the populace. They had come to make examples of areas of the population that rejected them—they had come to kill and destroy.

Little Andrea Roget was only three years old at the time, but she would remember the rapine and slaughter the Red soldiers inflicted on the innocent people. Disturbing dreams and nightmares would bring back the horrible incident even into her adulthood, and the girl would recall that day with horror and revulsion.

The first people to die were *Docteur* and *Madame* Roget. Shot down before their infant daughter's eyes, the little girl could barely comprehend what had happened to her parents. Then the slaughter was turned on the village men. Executed in groups, the piles of dead grew around the huts.

Then it was the women's turn for their specific lesson in Communist mercy and justice.

Hours of rape and torment went on before the females were herded together in one large group. The Soviet burp guns chattered like squawking birds of death as swarms of steel-jacketed 7.63 millimeter slugs slammed into living flesh.

Then the village was burned while the wounded who had survived the first fusillades were flung screaming into the flames. When they tried to climb out of the inferno, they met the bayonets of the "liberators."

Finally, after this last outrage, the Communist soldiery marched off singing the songs of their revolution.

It was several hours after the carnage that the French paratroopers showed up. They had received word of the crime from a young man who lived in a nearby village. He had come to see Dr. Roget regarding treatment for an ulcerated leg. After the youth had heard the shooting while approaching the hamlet, he'd left the main trail and approached in the cover offered by the jungle. Peering through the dense foliage, the young Indochinese perceived the horror and limped painfully on his bad leg fifty kilometers to the nearest military post.

The paratroopers, when they arrived, were shocked. These combat veterans had seen atrocities before. They had endured having their own people taken hostage to be executed by the Gestapo during the recent war in Europe. But even the savagery of the massacre of this inconsequential little village was of such magnitude they could scarcely believe their eyes.

The commanding officer looked around at the devastation and shook his head. *"Le SS peut prendre une leçon des cettes bêtes*—the SS could take a lesson from these beasts!"

The French *paras* searched through the smoking ruins, pulling the charred corpses out for a decent burial. One grizzled trooper, his face covered with three days' growth of beard, stumbled across little Andrea who had miraculously been overlooked during the murderous binge of the Viet Minh. He knelt down beside her, his tenderest feelings brought to the surface from the sight of the pathetic, beautiful child. He stroked her cheek gently, then took her in his brawny arms and stood up.

"Oh, *pauvre enfante*," he cooed to her. "We will take you away from all this *horreur*." The paratrooper carried the little girl through the ravaged village to the road where a convoy of secondhand U.S. Army trucks waited. These vehicles, barely useable, were kept running through the desperate inventiveness of mechanics who had only the barest essentials in the way of tools and parts. But, for the French who fought this thankless war, that was only par for the course.

Little Andrea sat in the lap of the commanding officer during the tedious trip into Hanoi. The column had to halt periodically to check the road ahead for mines. There was also an ambush by the Viet Minh in which the child was protected by being hidden in a ditch while the short but fierce battle was fought until the attackers broke off the fight and snuck away.

Upon arriving in Hanoi, the *paras* followed the usual procedure for war orphans and turned the girl over to a Catholic orphanage. This institution, run by the Soeurs de la Charité—the Sisters of Charity—did their best to check out Andrea's background. But all the records in the home village had been destroyed, and the child could say only her first name. She hadn't quite learned her last name, so all that could be garnered from her baby talk was the name "Andrea." She had inherited most of her looks from her mother, hence she had a decidedly Oriental appearance. The nuns did not know the girl had French blood. Thus Andrea Roget was given a Vietnamese name and became listed officially as Andrea Thuy.

Her remaining childhood at the orphanage was happy. She pushed the horrible memories of the Viet Minh raid back into her subconscious, concentrating on her new life. Andrea grew tall and beautiful, getting an excellent education and also learning responsibility and leadership. Parentless children were constantly showing up at the orphanage. Andrea, when she reached her teens, did her part in taking care of them. This important task was expanded from the normal care and feeding of the children to teaching school. Andrea was a brilliant student, and plans were being made to send her to France where she would undoubtedly be able to earn a university degree.

But Dien Bien Phu fell in 1954.

Once again, the war had touched her life with insidious

cruelty. The orphanage in Hanoi had to be closed when that city became part of Communist North Vietnam. The gentle Soeurs de la Charité took their charges and moved south to organize a new orphanage in Attopeu, Laos.

Despite this disruption in her education, Andrea did not stop growing physically and spiritually. She was a happy young girl, approaching womanhood, being loved and loving in return as she performed her tasks with the unfortunate waifs at the orphanage.

Then the Pathet Lao came.

These zealots made the Viet Minh look like Sunday school teachers. Wild, fanatical, and uncivilized, these devotees of Marxism knew no limits in their war making. Capable of unspeakable cruelty and displaying incredible savagery and stupidity, they were so terrible that they won not one convert in any of the areas they conquered.

Andrea was fifteen years old when the orphanage was raided. This time there was no chance for her to be overlooked or considered too inconsequential for torment. She, like all the older girls and the nuns, was ravished countless times in the screaming orgy. When the rapine finally ended, the Pathet Lao set the mission's buildings on fire. But this wasn't the end of their "fun."

The nuns, because they were Europeans, were murdered. Naked, raped, and shamed, the pitiable women were flung alive into the flames. This same outrage, as committed by the Viet Minh in her old village, awakened the memory of the terrible event for Andrea. She went into shock as the murder of the nuns continued.

Some screamed, but most prayed, as they endured their horrible deaths. Andrea, whose Oriental features still overshadowed her French ancestry, was thought to be just another native orphan.

She endured one more round of raping with the other girls, then the Pathet Lao, having scored another victory for Communism, gathered up their gear and loot to march away to the next site in their campaign of Marxist expansionism.

Andrea gathered the surviving children around her. With the nuns now gone, she was the leader of their pathetic group. Instinct told her to move south. To the north were the Red marauders and their homeland. Whatever lay in the opposite direction had to be better. She could barely remember the gruff kindness of the French paratroopers, but she did recall they went south. Andrea didn't know if these same men would be there or not, but it was worth the effort.

The journey she took the other children on was long and arduous. Short of food, the little column moved south through the jungle eating wild fruit and other vegetation. For two weeks Andrea tended her flock, sometimes carrying a little one until her arms ached with the effort. She comforted them and soothed their fears as best she could. She kept up their hope by telling them of the kind people who awaited them at the end of the long trail.

Two weeks after leaving the orphanage, Andrea sighted a patrol of soldiers. Her first reaction was of fear and alarm, but the situation of the children was so desperate that she had to take a chance and contact the troops. After making sure the children had concealed themselves in the dense foliage, Andrea approached the soldiers. If they were going to rape her, she figured, they would have their fun but never know the orphans were concealed nearby. Timidly, the young girl moved out onto the trail in front of them. With her lips trembling, she bowed and spoke softly.

"*Chao ong.*"

The lead soldier, startled by her unexpected appearance, had almost shot her. He relaxed a bit as he directed his friends to watch the surrounding jungle in case this was part of an insidious Viet Cong trick. He smiled back at the girl. "*Chao co.* What can I do for you?"

Andrea swallowed nervously but felt better when she noted there was no red star insignia on his uniform. Then she launched into a spiel about the nuns, the orphanage—everything. When the other soldiers approached and quite obviously meant her no harm, she breathed a quiet pray of thanks under her breath.

She and the children were safe at last.

These troops, who were from the South Vietnamese army, took the little refugees back to their detachment commander. This young lieutenant followed standard practice for such situations and made arrangements to transport Andrea and her charges farther back to higher headquarters for interrogation and eventual relocation in a safe area.

Andrea was given a thorough interview with a South Vietnamese intelligence officer. He was pleased to learn that the girl was not only well acquainted with areas now under occupation by Communist troops but was also fluent in the Vietnamese, Laotian, and French languages. He passed this information on to other members of his headquarters staff for discussion as to Andrea's potential as an agent. After a lengthy conversation among themselves, it was agreed to keep her in the garrison after sending the other orphans to Saigon.

Andrea waited there while a complete background investigation was conducted on her past life. They delved so deeply into the information available on her that each item of intelligence seemed to lead to another until they discovered the truth that even she didn't know. She was a Eurasian, and her father was a Frenchman—*Monsieur le Docteur* Gaston Roget.

This led to the girl's being taken to an even higher ranking officer for her final phase of questioning. He was a kindly appearing colonel who saw to it that the girl was given her favorite cold drink—an iced Coca-Cola—before he began speaking with her.

"You have seen much of Communism, Andrea," he said. "Tell me, *ma chere*, what is your opinion of the Viet Minh, Viet Cong, and Pathet Lao?"

Andrea took a sip of her drink then pointed at the man's pistol in the holster on his hip. "Let me have your gun, *monsieur*, and I will kill every one of them!"

"I'm afraid that would be impossible," the colonel said. "Even a big soldier could not kill all of them by himself. But there is another way you can fight them."

Andrea, eager, leaned forward. "How, *monsieur*?"

"You have some very unusual talents and bits of knowledge, Andrea," the colonel said. "Those things, when combined with others that we could teach you, would make you a most effective fighter against the Communists."

"What could you teach me, *monsieur*?" Andrea asked.

"Well, for example, you know three languages. Would you like to learn more? Tai, Chinese, possibly English?"

"If that would help me kill Pathet Lao and Viet Cong," Andrea said, "then I want to learn. But I don't understand how that would do anything to destroy those Red devils."

"They would be skills you could learn—along with others—that would enable you to go into their midst and do mischief and harm to them," the colonel said. "But learning these things would be difficult and unpleasant at times."

"What could be more difficult and more unpleasant than what I've already been through?" Andrea asked.

"A good point," the colonel said. He recognized the maturity in the young girl and decided to speak to her as an adult. "When would you like to begin this new phase of your education, *mademoiselle*?"

"Now! Today!" Andrea cried getting to her feet.

"I am sorry, *mademoiselle*," the colonel said with a smile. "You will have to wait until tomorrow morning."

The next day's training was the first part of two solid years of intensified schooling. Because of being able to mask her true identity, South Vietnamese intelligence decided to have her retain the name Thuy—as the Soeurs de la Charité had named her.

Andrea acquired more languages along with unusual skills necessary in the dangerous profession she had chosen for herself. Besides disguises and a practice at mimicking various accents and dialects, the fast-maturing girl picked up various methods of how to kill people. These included poisons and drugs, easily concealable weapons, and the less subtle methods of blowing an adversary to bits with plastic explosives. After each long day of training, Andrea concluded her schedule by poring over books of mug shots showing the faces and identities of Communist leaders and officials up in the north.

Finally, with her deadly education completed, seventeen-year-old Andrea Thuy *née* Roget, went out into the cold.

During two years of operations, she assassinated four top Red bigwigs. Her devotion to their destruction was to the extent that she was even willing to use her body if it would lower their guard and aid her in gaining their confidence. Once that was done, Andrea displayed absolutely no reluctance in administering the *coup de grace* to put an end to their efforts at spreading world socialism.

When the American involvement in South Vietnam stepped up, a Central Intelligence Agency case officer named Clayton Andrews learned of this unusual young woman and her deadly talents. Andrews had been tasked with creating an elite killer/raider outfit. After learning of Andrea, he knew he wanted her to be a part of this crack team. Using his influence and talents of persuasion, he saw to it that the beautiful female operative was sent to Langely Air Force Base in Virginia to the special CIA school located there.

When the Americans finished honing her fangs at Langely, she returned to South Vietnam and was put into another job category. Commissioned a lieutenant in the ARVN, she was appointed a temporary major and assigned to Special Operation Group's Black Eagles Detachment which was under the command of Robert Falconi.

Andrea accompanied the Black Eagles on their first mission. This operation, named Hanoi Hellground, was a direct action type against a Red whorehouse and pleasure palace deep within North Vietnam. Andrea participated in the deadly combat that resulted, killing her share of the Red enemy in the firefights that erupted in the green hell of the jungle. There was not a Black Eagle who would deny she had been superlative in the performance of her duties.

But she soon fell out of grace.

Not because of cowardice, sloppy work, or inefficiency, but because of that one thing that could disarm any woman—love. She went head-over-heels into it with Robert Falconi.

Clayton Andrews was promoted upstairs, and his place was taken by another CIA case officer. This one, named Chuck Fagin, found he had inherited a damned good outfit except that its commander and one of the operatives were involved in a red-hot romance. An emotional entanglement like that spelled disaster with a capital D in the espionage and intelligence business.

Fagin had no choice but to pull Andrea out of active ops. He had her put in his office as the administrative director. Andrea knew that the decision was the right one. She would have done the same thing. She or Falconi might have lost their heads and pulled something emotional or thoughtless if either one had suddenly been placed into a dangerous situation. That sort of illogical condition could have resulted not only in their own deaths but to the demise of other Black Eagles as well. At times, a dedicated operative had to be tough on herself.

It was only a few short hours after her interview with Chuck Fagin that Andrea Thuy was prepared for her new mission.

Her entry into the war zone was certainly going to be unusual. Not only would it call for great care and bravery on her part but her skills as an actress and mimic would be stretched to the limit.

But, unlike a poor performance on the stage, she would get more than boos and catcalls from the audience. In this case, they would demonstrate their displeasure in a much more negative manner:

They would kill her—and probably each and every Black Eagle, too.

CHAPTER SEVEN

Major Falconi strolled slowly among the various instructional groups. Both the Alpha and Bravo fire teams were involved in teaching the Pings to use the M16 rifles they had brought in for the Chinese mercenaries. The eager students, squatting around ponchos spread out on the ground on which the weapons were laid, drank in every word of their Black Eagle instructors.

The classes were being given at the edge of the jungle adjacent to the same rice paddies the Black Eagles had used for a drop zone.

In the past, Tsang's men had been armed with a variety of weapons that had included some American M1 rifles and M2 carbines acquired under very suspicious circumstances from the South Vietnamese army. Other models in their arsenal included the usual stuff taken from dead VC, a lot of French surplus left over from former colonial times, and even a Japanese Ariska rifle or two that had been used in World War II.

Naturally, under such conditions, ammo supply had been a nightmare for Tsang. At various times, he and his men had been forced to trade off weapons among themselves, or even use less desirable ones because the bullets available dictated what could be taken out on an operation.

But now things were different.

With all the men carrying M16s and using the same 5.56 millimeter ammunition, the Pings could count on a hundred percent muster for each mission.

The Black Eagles found their unusual students enthusiastic and skilled. A rudimentary firing range involving silhouette targets had been set up. The Chinese riflemen had no trouble putting their shots into the killing zones. The only problem was the mechanical side of the instruction. Like most people not used to the M16s, the Pings showed a tendency to use too much oil on them. The weapons were not too forgiving of such treatment. Especially when a gooey-dirt layer built up in the moving parts of the rifles.

Falconi stood in the shade of a tall tree, watching the groups of his men taking the Pings through the field-stripping procedure necessary to clean the rifles. He watched casually, feeling relaxed and easy as he noted how fast the Chinese mercs seemed to be learning.

"Skipper!"

Falconi glanced up to see Sparks Martin hurrying toward him. When the Navy man arrived, he spoke softly to his commander. "ETA in fifteen minutes."

"Roger," Falconi said, checking his watch.

Sparks abruptly left to return to the commo shack he had set up for the larger radio. Falconi waited a couple of minutes and moved out toward the rice paddies, seemingly to look at the instruction from another angle.

After a few minutes he could barely hear the sound of an aircraft flying at an extremely high altitude. Falconi had to move away from the sound of the instructors' voices to make sure his ears weren't playing tricks on him. Again, he glanced at his watch, then turned his eyes upward.

Several of the Pings noticed what he was doing and

made some comments. Bullhorn Maywood, in the middle of slapping his weapon back together, knew exactly what was going on. And he, like the other Black Eagles, was very much aware of what was expected of him. He called over to Falconi in his loud voice, "What the hell you lookin' at, skipper?"

"I hear a strange airplane way—way up there."

Tsang, the Ping's captain, walked away from his group. "Is it American?"

"We're not supposed to have any flyovers in this operational area," Falconi said, lying. "I don't know whose it is."

Now Tsang peered skyward, his eyes trying to perceive the aircraft. "I hear it good now. But don't see something, oh-you-kid."

Falconi's eyes finally made out the distant dot in the sky. "There it is. But I can't tell what kind it is."

Top Gordon joined the two. "I don't recognize the sound of that engine."

"Maybe it Russian or Chinese," Tsang suggested.

"Nope," Falconi said. "I've heard every type of Communist airplane there is."

Tsang was astounded. "Really?"

"You bet he has," Top Gordon says. "That's how he made major."

"Oh!" Tsang said impressed.

"And it's not American," Falconi continued. "That engine is very unfamiliar to me." He gave Tsang a meaningful look. "It's kind of scary."

"Yeah?"

"Yeah. Almost like it was a ghost airplane—or one that is certainly not from this mortal world."

Tsang, brave beyond belief in battle, swallowed nervously. "Such things, or even speaking of them, make my blood turn cold, oh-you-kid!"

Falconi displayed a worried frown. "Me too!"

"There are as many strange spirits in sky as there are in deep part of jungle," Tsang added.

"Look!" Top said. "Something's fallen out of it!"

Sure enough, and even smaller dot was behind the airplane that now continued on its way away from the area. The thing that fell was at and incredible altitude.

"Maybe it bomb!" Tsang said. "Atomic bomb!"

"Naw," Top assured him. "Nobody's going to waste an atomic bomb on those rice paddies."

"I guess not," Tsang said.

The thing fell toward them for another three minutes, until Falconi finally exclaimed. "It's a parachutist!"

Then it became apparent to the crowd watching as they could make out the spread arms and legs. The person continued to fall farther, until blossoming material finally erupted from the form. It opened sharply to evolve into a parachute canopy.

"Now we'll see who it is," Top said.

"There's definitely something unusual about this," Falconi said. "I can't quite figure it out, but that parachutist is not a regular person."

"You mean not human, oh-you-kid?" Tsang asked a bit agitated.

"Who knows?" the Falcon responded mysteriously.

The jumper, utilizing a colorful slit canopy, steered toward them. Tsang, continuing to watch closely, grew excited. "Look! The parachute is Ping-Yan-Uen colors— yellow and black."

Now the Ping women and children had come from the village to observe the strange happening. They weren't sure what was going on but knew whatever it was, an exotic occurrence seemed to be taking place.

The jumper continued his descent, carefully using the high steering capability of the parachute to avoid landing in the rice paddies. And when he did hit the ground by the edge of the jungle, he was able to sit down lightly without having to make the crashing roll that would have been necessary had he been using a T10 parachute.

The crowd, with the Black Eagles and the Ping soldiers in the lead, hurried over to the new arrival. The jumper quickly shucked chute, equipment, and helmet, then fetched a rifle, holding it high over his head.

The crowd ran up and stopped. They stared in gape-mouthed wonder at this jumper who faced them.

The parachutist was a beautiful woman.

"Wai," Andrea Thuy said. *"Pin-ko hai Shiu-Wai?"*

Tsang held up his hand. *"Ngoh hai Shiu-Wai!"*

"Where did you come from?" Falconi asked.

"I do not know," Andrea answered.

"You speak English, too?" Tsang asked her astounded. *"Nei kiu-tso mi-ye meng a?"*

"I do not know my name," Andrea said. "But I know why I am here."

"Tell us then," Falconi demanded.

"I have come to fight with the Ping-Yan-Uen," Andrea said.

There was a long, confused silence until Tsang finally reacted. "Aaiiieee!" he shrieked. "You are Chin-Sza-Tung—Warrior-Sister!" He turned to his people, his face contorted with awe and fear. "Chin-Sza-Tung!" He fell to the ground, prostrating himself in front of Andrea. The other Pings did the same, setting up a fearful moaning as they covered their eyes, not daring to look directly at this living goddess.

Andrea winked at Falconi, then spoke aloud to the people. "I cannot say that I am Warrior-Sister. I do not know anything of myself, except that I am here to help you fight."

"Yes! Yes!" Tsang exclaimed. "You are Chin—Sza-Tung!"

"I do not say that! I cannot prove that!" Andrea insisted. "And I seek men who bear the name of killer birds."

The major took his cue. "I am called Falconi—the

95

Falcon. And my men are known as the Black Eagles."

"Yes," Andrea said. "I seek you. For you, too, are here with the Ping-Yan-Uen to work as my instruments."

Falconi bowed. "We are at your service, Warrior-Sister."

"I cannot say I am Warrior-Sister," Andrea repeated. "But I would talk with you first. Then with the *Shiu-Wai*."

Tsang, a brave man in any combat situation, cringed in fear at the thought of conversation with a goddess. But he answered in a quaking voice, "Summon me when you wish my humble presence, Chin-Sza-Tung!"

"I cannot say I am Warrior-Sister!" Andrea motioned to Falconi and led him away from the crowd into the jungle. They walked into the vegetation for twenty meters before stopping. The young Eurasian woman turned and smiled at him. "How do you think it's going?"

"Quite well," Falconi answered. "But you keep denying you're the Warrior-Sister. I told Fagin you should claim to be that goddess."

Andrea shook her head. "Fagin became extremely concerned about trying to pull off something like this," she explained. "He called in an expert on Far East psychology and another on their religions. It was decided that I should give all the appearances of being Chin-Sza-Tung, but to never openly claim to be. That way, if my mortality becomes evident, we can always remind the Ping-Yan-Uen that I never told them I was their goddess."

"I see," Falconi said. "If you're wounded or killed, it would sort of ruin the picture of your personal holiness, wouldn't it?"

"Yes," Andrea replied. "And in that case, you are to tell the Ping-Yan-Uen that I was a messenger for Warrior-Sister."

"Good idea," Falconi said. "In the meantime, I'll instruct the men to refrain from making a big deal over you being a diety, yet treat you like you truly are."

"It'll be tricky and dangerous," Andrea warned him.

Falconi nodded. "In the meantime, what's the latest poop from group?"

"Both ARVN GHQ and MAC V want this area completely pacified as quickly as possible," Andrea said. "The plan is to construct several good-sized fortified hamlets and bring in villagers and militia from other areas more difficult to control."

Falconi shrugged. "That was in our original OPLAN anyhow."

"Yes," Andrea answered. "But the importance of this area has increased in only the previous twenty-four hours. The project is top secret. The powers that be have decided to also put in a strong fire base here complete with heavy artillery and airstrips. This location is close enough to both North Vietnam and Laos that a major part of this war can be directed out of the Pings' territory."

"Right. Now how are we to carry out this thing?"

Andrea smiled. "I'm supposed to be in charge. We're to figure out a way that you can pass on tactical decisions to me."

"That's easy enough. I'll make suggestions and you act on them," Falconi said. "If Tsang comes up with an idea I approve, I'll scratch myself above the neck somewhere—nose, ears, or throat, for example. If I disagree with him, I'll clear my throat. How's that?"

"I understand," Andrea said. "I'm really not expecting any problems. We should be able to have this area pacified in a relatively short time."

"And with a minimum of casualties among the Pings," Falcon said. "That's the bottom line. These little guys are great, and I admire them. But they're too damned eager to die in battle to suit me."

"I'll work on that, too," Andrea said.

Falconi nodded. "Well, let's get back to the others and get the show on the road."

The two walked back toward the clearing where the other Black Eagles and the Ping-Yan-Uen waited.

Lieutenant Colonel Krashchenko looked up as the knock on the door interrupted his work. *"Da?"*

A message clerk entered and saluted. *"Chao ong, Trung Ta."*

Krashchenko, who didn't understand what had been said—and didn't give a damn either—returned the salute and accepted the canvas pouch left on his desk. He waited until the visitor made an exit, then opened the container and pulled out the messages there. All were written in Major Truong's careful Russian script, having been translated from Vietnamese into Krashchenko's native language. This intelligence had been judged to be potential operations of the Black Eagles. It was up to the KGB colonel to make the final determination.

Krashchenko was glad Truong had stayed away after completing the task. The time he spent with the NVA major was becoming even more unpleasant for him.

The missives told of several combat engagements involving a cadre of American military personnel and either ARVN troops or local militia. The first couple could not possibly have been the Black Eagles, so Krashchenko immediately discarded them.

But the others were more interesting.

There was one attack on a VC supply base west of Saigon. This one looked rather suspicious since inside information had to be involved. Krashchenko took a grease pencil and marked the spot on the acetate covering of his wall map.

The second example with potential importance involved a surprise capture of a Red hospital base. This occurred in an area northeast of Muang Khammouan. Krashchenko started to mark that one, too, but something in his bureaucratic mind reminded him of some obscure bit of information in his files. He went to his desk and pulled out a stack of manila folders. After rifling through them, he removed one and opened it. He'd been right. A small Viet Cong medical detachment had been cut off during patrol actions. No doubt one or more of them had been captured and talked, spilling the location of the hospital to ARVN intelligence. Therefore, Krashchenko decided not to include that one as a potential Black Eagles mission.

The third incident involved probing actions off Highway One between Da Nang and Dong Ha. That showed a distinct possibility, too. He marked the area down and turned to the last report.

The local VC commander situated in an area in the northwest part of South Vietnam between Kontum and the Laotian border had sent in an interesting bit of intelligence. The officer reported a detachment of Americans had parachuted into the territory and linked up with the Chinese mercenary group known as the Ping-Yan-Uen. There had been a minor skirmish, but no overt actions since.

Krashchenko entered the intelligence on his map and stepped back to study it.

His first, most basic impression was that an A-detachment of Special Forces had gone into the area to supply and direct the Ping-Yan-Uen in a normal, unremarkable campaign as a small part of the counterinsurgency efforts that were spread all over South Vietnam.

But something clicked in the KGB officer's mind. He couldn't quite justify his initial suspicions, but his instincts told him that there was more here than met the eye. Despite the fact the area was rather unremarkable, the stamp of Robert Falconi and the Black Eagles seemed to be very prominent.

Krashchenko made a quick mental evaluation.

The Americans had infiltrated by parachute. Why? Was there some rush? It was a relatively safe place. The Viet Cong there were only a small group. The villagers had either fled south or had been forcibly removed to other areas by the South Vietnamese government. There was nothing but abandoned rice paddies and a couple of small jungle hamlets that were beginning to disintegrate from no longer being inhabited or cared for.

Krashchenko spoke aloud. "Why would the *Amerikanets* go in there?" He tried to put himself in the place of a commander conducting anti-guerrilla operations. There were other operational areas that would seem to require much more and quicker attention. This particular place could be forgotten and ignored for months without any undue consequences.

Suddenly Krashchenko laughed aloud. Here was a logical area from where intercept missions or even open assaults were launched into both North Vietnam or Laos. The potential could not be denied. He stepped forward and drew a big circle around the territory.

At the same time, the door opened and Major Truong stepped into the office. He smiled wryly at his Russian counterpart. "What is so funny, Comrade Lieutenant Colonel Krashchenko? Are you drawing comical pictures on your map?"

Krashchenko suddenly feeling confident, whirled and faced the man who had become his tormentor. "That is not a cartoon, comrade," he said indicating the circle, "it is a noose—one that will soon be slipped over Maj. Robert Falconi's neck!"

*　　　*　　　*

Flickering light from small lamps lit the interior of the hut. Only three people, kneeling around a low Japanese tea table, were present.

Robert Falconi, leader of the Black Eagles; Tsang, leader of the Ping-Yan-Uen; and Andrea Thuy, also known as Warrior-Sister or Chin-Sza-Tung, sipped hot tea as they planned their future fighting strategy.

"You are our Warrior-Sister!" Tsang insisted for the dozenth time.

"I cannot truthfully say that I am," Andrea said. "But, if you wish to call me by that name, please do so." She looked at Falconi. "You also. I am not offended by the appellation."

"Thank you," Falconi replied.

"You must be the Warrior-Sister!" Tsang said. "You come from the sky."

"By parachute," Andrea reminded him.

"Just like my men and me," Falconi said.

"But you are men—*men!*" Tsang said. "And she is woman. A beautiful woman who is soldier." He looked reverently and lovingly at Andrea. "You are soldier, *tsing nei.*"

"Yes," Andrea answered truthfully. "I am a soldier."

"A soldier and a beautiful woman," Tsang said. "Which is what our religion teaches us. The old legends say nothing of how you to come. Whether to float like ghost, fly with wings, or with big parachute. Only that you come to Ping-Yan-Uen from sky." He bowed respectfully toward the woman. "We will follow you. You are our leader."

"I will let you lead my men, too," Falconi said.

"Thank you," Andrea said. "But you both must remember that I cannot guarantee who I am."

"What is it we must do?" Tsang asked again ignoring her protestations. "*Tsing nei*, Chin-Sza-Tung!"

Andrea, who had already spoken of the tactical requirements with Falconi, looked directly at the Ping's leader. "We must go to the base camp of the VC and destroy them."

Tsang's face broke into a wide grin. *"Gaaung-Po!* There will be two great battles."

"Two?" Falconi asked.

"Yes," Tsang answered. "Viet Cong have two hamlets. One is advance post to watch us. Other is main one."

"Then we will attack them one at a time," Falconi said. "The local VC are so weak there is no need for fancy strategy."

Andrea looked at Tsang. "But we must not waste men's lives."

"But the Ping-Yan-Uen soldiers would be honored to die in battle under Warrior-Sister!" Tsang protested. "No better way to become general."

"I do not want to send too many of our men to the generals," Andrea said.

"But—"

"I am commanding, thus!" Andrea said sharply.

Tsang's expression showed his humility. "I am sorry, Chin-Sza-Tung! I will tell the men that Warrior-Sister wants them to be careful and try to live through the battles." Suddenly his face lit up. "Ah! Now I understand. We will need all the men possible when we conquer China."

Andrea repeated herself. "I do not want the men to be reckless. I will be disenchanted."

"Of course, Chin-Sza-Tung," Tsang said. "I will personally see to it that you are obeyed."

Andrea pointed to Falconi. "And that includes your Black Eagles too, Major Falconi."

"As you wish, Warrior-Sister."

Lieutenant Trun, the adjutant of the special Viet Cong battalion, came instantly awake as the young guerrilla

102

shook him. *"Ai do?"*

"I am the headquarters messenger, comrade *Thieu Uy*," the man said. "You are to report there immediately. Comrade *Thieu Ta* Dnang has sent me for you."

Trun rolled from his sleeping mat and scurried through the mosquito netting. After quickly climbing into his uniform and slipping his feet into the heavy-soled sandals, he rushed out of the sleeping hut. Trun sprinted across the hamlet to battalion headquarters.

Major Dnang looked up at his entrance. "A message has just arrived, Comrade Trun."

The young man was red-faced with embarrassment. "I am sorry to have been asleep, comrade," he said.

Dnang smiled. "Even an eager *thieu uy* like you must take out time to rest," he said in understanding.

"Cam on ong, comrade major," Trun said. "What is the information we have received?"

"We have been placed on an alert status by G two in Hanoi," Dnang said.

"Then we are being committed to combat?"

Dnang shook his head. "Not yet. But we must be ready. I therefore want you to muster the battalion immediately."

Trun saluted, then rushed to the porch. A single, hollowed-out steel pipe hung there. The young adjutant grabbed a wooden mallet attached to it and began banging on the device as hard as he could.

In only seconds, the entire battalion came awake and rushed out into the darkness of their small garrison. Despite being sleep-numbed and fatigued, they formed up quickly and properly. A few terse orders were barked and a quick roll taken. Trun stepped off the porch and took the reports of the company commanders, then he turned and waited for Major Dnang to make his appearance.

Dnang stepped from the headquarters and descended

103

the rickety steps from the porch. He walked to a point directly in front of Trun.

Trun saluted sharply. "Comrade *Thieu Ta*! The battalion is all present and accounted for."

Dnang returned the salute, gazing at his command with undisguised pride and admiration. *"Chao ong, nguoi linh!* We are now alerted for possible insertion into a combat zone. You have spent long weeks preparing for this coming mission. Every man has a full issue of ammunition and grenades. Your weapons, rations, and other gear have been kept packed and ready to go. If G two in Hanoi gives us the signal to seek combat with the American gangsters, you will be ready to destroy them!"

A wild cheer erupted from the men. It was carefully orchestrated by the veteran company commanders.

"I can say in complete confidence that this bandit Falconi and his gang of Black Eagles have never, *never* met as formidable a group of fighters as yourselves. Victory is ours. The Americans will be crushed by the crushing tides of your courage and determination."

Trun faced the assembled troops and raised both arms above his head. "Long live the socialist revolution!"

The men imitated him, their cries of "Long live the socialist revolution!" echoing across their formation.

"Long live the socialist revolution!" Trun repeated as if anxious to get the point across.

"Long live the socialist revolution!" the men cried back.

Dnang smiled to himself and listened once again to the wild cheering of his men. His thoughts were interrupted by the arrival of his headquarters orderly.

"Comrade *Thieu Ta* Dnang," he said excitedly. "Another message has come. We are committed!"

CHAPTER EIGHT

The jungle was quiet. The silence proclaimed that special time of rest when even the violent world of nature's kill-or-be-killed doctrine was suspended for a brief half hour or so.

This was the early dawn. It was no longer night, yet day hadn't made enough of an appearance to cause any inroads into the inky blackness. The beasts that killed and fed by night were back in their lairs, exhausted from the efforts they had expended in the previous few hours. A few had full bellies that digested the unfortunates who hadn't been quick enough to avoid their savage attacks. Most, however, felt hunger, and the next night's forays would find them more vicious, with all skills honed sharp in the most driving killing instinct of them all: that which is motivated by hunger.

Archie Dobbs wasn't hungry.

But his intentions at that particular moment were as deadly as any hunting tiger's. The Black Eagles' scout, his knife ready in his right hand, stepped gingerly through the jungle vegetation and deadfall that littered the ground. Before each step he took, the scout carefully felt what was under each boot. Then, leaning forward and putting his full weight on it, he continued his slow, deadly trek. A twig or dry leaf would crackle ominously loud in this dark silence. When Archie was convinced there was nothing to give him away, he would slowly bring the other foot forward in this stealthy walk he made toward the object of his death-dealing intentions.

The Viet Cong sentry dozed carelessly at his post.

His was the last stint before the normal day's duty began, and he dreamily thought of the breakfast of hot rice and tea that awaited him in the base camp only a scant few meters behind his position. His comrades in other guerrilla units farther south were involved in a growing conflict with the Americans. But the war zone in this particular area seemed rather quiet. It was true that a detachment of capitalist gangsters had arrived a couple of days ago to augment the Chinese bandits that he and his friends fought from time to time, but that event didn't seem to make things more serious in this particular area. The situation still seemed rather easy and slow despite the intrusions of these large strangers.

The young communist's eyes popped open in full wakefulness as the arm clamped tight around his throat cutting off his wind. Then there were several, swift ice-hot sensations into his back. He could feel metal bite deep into his innards, and the wheeze of his suddenly collapsed right lung was like the sigh of a village maiden. His knees weakened, and his mind clouded over as the fluid drained from his body.

Archie Dobbs slammed the knife in one more time for good measure. He could feel the slow give of muscle and tissue with each bite of the blade and the warm stickiness of blood all over his hand. The body, which had stiffened against him, suddenly shuddered and went limp. Archie had to abandon his grip on the knife in order to slowly lower his victim's body softly to the ground in order to avoid undue noise.

The scout turned and motioned through the trees.

Robert Falconi, in the company of Andrea Thuy and Tsang, noted Archie's hand signal. He spoke softly into his radio. "This is Falcon. Execute. Execute. Execute. Out."

Top Gordon, on the left flank of the attack, slung his Prick-Six radio over his shoulder and, at the same time, brought the muzzle of his M16 up. He squeezed the trigger, sending several fire bursts of 5.56 millimeter bullets slicing through the vegetation into the VC camp on the other side of the bushes where he and his men were concealed.

The Pings among the Alphas sprang forward at the sudden shots. They leaped through the vegetation and charged into the opening of the camp, their battle cry eerie in the early morning air.

"Gaaung-Po! Gaaung-Po!"

Startled VC responded slowly—too slowly for their own good. The first ones up, stupid with sleep and confusion, stumbled into the incoming rounds that flung them back onto their sleeping mats like jerking puppets whose strings had been cut.

Others, with a more warlike instinct, leaped to their feet fighting. Their Chinese and Russian weapons sparked in the dim light. But without specific targets, the rounds they fired merely clipped jungle brush or flew off into the dark sky.

The Alpha's target was a series of huts marking the east side of the village. Calvin Culpepper, Bullhorn Maywood, and Toby Barker, each with a trio of Pings at his command, swept down onto their objective. The combined firing was done in short, controlled bursts with three or four 5.56 millimeter slugs slapping into the human targets exposed to their lethal attention.

"Down!" Top yelled. He pulled a grenade from his harness and sent it hurtling toward the large, thatched roof of the middle hut. Before it hit the palm leaves covering the structure, a second was hurled right behind it.

Both went through the flimsy ceiling and bounced once off the dirt floor before exploding. Slices of shrapnel sent sparks flying milliseconds before punching into the writhing bodies of the Viet Cong.

Then, with M16s barking death, the Alphas threw out their own curtain of flying slugs as they moved in to secure their objective.

On the other side of the camp, Chun Kim and his Bravo Fire Team were having more difficulties. An unsuspected VC machine gun nest was located under the raised floor of the farthest hut assigned for them to take.

The crew there, who evidently slept with their weapons, had been awakened by the initial shooting, and they had responded quickly.

Dozens of 7.62 rounds from the Russian Goryunov heavy machine gun flew into the Bravos' battle formation. A couple of unfortunate Pings, farther forward than the rest, caught the full loads waist high. One, screaming in a combination of pain and rage, writhed under the pounding of the slugs, going down to the ground in a twisting fall. His companion, hit by a close cluster of the bullets, was blown into two pieces, his legs still continuing toward the target as the upper part of the torso crashed into the dirt.

"Back! Back!" Kim yelled.

The others began withdrawing while at the same time laying down enough fire to cause the machine gunners to duck back into their hole. But not fast enough to avoid another casualty among the Pings. This one, a young soldier, had paused long enough to attempt a carefully aimed shot.

The VC crew sent a swarm of slugs that hit knee, thigh, midsection, and chest almost simultaneously. The brave youth was thrown five meters backward from the impact.

He hit the ground, bloodied and torn, rolling over once before stopping. The Ping had been cold-dead on the first bounce.

Kim, ever the heavy weapons infantryman, always kept a grenade launcher in his combat gear. The M79 only wighed five point ninety-five pounds, and each 40 millimeter round tipped the scales at a mere eight ounces. For a stocky Korean who had been raised as a farmboy in a country without modern conveniences or vehicles, lugging around a combat load like that was nothing.

Kim opened the launcher and deftly inserted a grenade.

"Watch it!" Blue Richards cried. The VC machine gun crew had popped up once again and raked their position. Luckily, only twigs and dirt flew up as the rounds missed the living targets.

Kim took careful aim and fired the launcher. His angle of attack, limited by raised ground to his immediate front, was too great. The grenade streaked through the hut above the machine gun and exploded behind it.

"Damn!" Kim yelled in rage. He tried to move to a better position but couldn't do much.

"Hey, Kim!" the Tripper yelled. "Load that mother and toss her over here."

"You bet!" Kim cracked the M79 again, slipping in another grenade. He rolled over, then sent the weapon hurtling through the air where the Tripper was situated.

The supply sergeant leaped quickly, catching the launcher, then crashed back to the ground as the 7.72 slugs from the enemy firing position sung in the air around his ears.

"You want extra rounds?" Kim hollered over at him.

"What the hell for? I already got one," the Tripper answered. "There ain't nothin' but a single gun to go after." He quickly scanned the automatic weapon's position. "Somebody give me some covering fire!"

Ray Swift Elk, situated on the right flank of their attack, rose up slightly and squeezed off a long fire burst of eight rounds. Then he ducked back down.

The Red gunner, infuriated by this show of disrespect, swung the muzzle of the Garyunov toward the Sioux Indian. He fired a series of bursts that came so close their concussions made Swift Elk's ears ring.

At that time, the Tripper leaped to his feet. Despite being plump as hell with a beer belly that hung over his pistol belt, he could move amazingly fast. Looking like a close-clipped Santa Claus who had just stepped out of a basic-training barber shop, he streaked off toward a better firing position for the grenade launcher.

The Viet Cong gunner saw him and shrieked in rage at what he considered a misplaced old man. *"Xin ong doi mot chut, Chu anh!"*

The Tripper, fat and fast, with bullets flying around his corpulent body, finally reached the safety of a fallen palm tree. He dove behind as splinters flew in angry explosions from the trunk.

"Hey, Tripper! You okay?" Blue Richards called.

The Tripper took off his cap and wiped at his perspiring, bald head. "Yeah! No problem!"

"Man!" Blue marveled loudly. "Yo're one fast sumbitch, you fat ol' fart! I'd love to use you to steal watermelons back home."

Tripper, declining any more commentary, edged toward the end of the tree. Fire from the machine gun still raked his position periodically, and it pissed him off. He took a deep breath and bellowed. "Do you fuckers mind givin' him somethin' to shoot at beside me?"

"Aw, hell," came back Blue's voice. "We don't mind a bit, Tripper."

Kim, Blue, and Swift Elk immediately set up a rapid, though badly aimed fusillade, at the machine gun nest. The Pings, assigned to the Bravos, knew enough English

110

to understand exactly what was going on. They added their own contribution to the din of shooting. Although unable to be accurate, the impromptu volleys came close enough at times to make the VC worry a bit.

Then the Tripper made his move.

He leaped up from his cover, ran forward and flung himself into a low-lying area of ground. He hit the dirt, rolled over and took a sight picture that showed the underside of the Viet Cong hut.

At the same time, the Red gunners sighted him. They pivoted their gun and fired.

Ignoring the Russian bullets flying around him, the Tripper cut loose. The launcher slammed back into his shoulder.

The little grenade streaked outward, slapped a bit of dirt, then went straight into the floor directly above the machine gun nest. The floor forced both the concussion and shrapnel downward, the whole effect slamming into the VC manning the firing post.

"Get 'em!" Kim yelled leaping to his feet and advancing.

"Gaaung-Po! Gaaung-Po!" the Pings yelled.

Ray Swift Elk added a warrior battle cry to the shouting, while Blue Richards contributed a shrill rebel yell.

The Tripper, on the other hand, slowly got to his feet and strolled to the objective in his clumsy waddle. He reached it at the same time as his charging companions. "Ain't no need to rush," he said calmly.

Blue slid under the hut and peered into the machine gun nest at the pulpy remnants of the crew. "Shit-far! Them fellars look like they been run through a meat grinder!" he exclaimed crawling back out into the open.

"They did," the Tripper said tossing Kim's grenade launcher back to him. "An M seventy-nine meat grinder."

111

"Way to go," Kim said. "I put you in for silver star, Tripper."

"I already got one of them things," the Tripper said. "How's about lettin' me have the pork and beans outta your C rations instead?"

"Fuck you!" Kim said. Among the Black Eagles, the pork and beans—along with pound cake and fruit cocktail—were considered gourmet delights when it came to eating in the field.

"Awright," the Tripper said. "I'll take the medal if that's the best you'll do for me."

Top Gordon, his Alphas having now swept through their objective, showed up on the Bravos' left flank. "Hey!" he yelled down to them. "You guys go on strike or something? This village isn't exactly secure yet! How about joining us, huh?"

Kim, ever the polite Oriental, bowed and smiled. "We thank you for kind invitation. Lead the way, Top."

Within a scant two minutes, both Alphas and Bravos—along with their Ping contingents—were formed up and moving forward toward the farthest edge of the objective.

Meanwhile, the Falcon and his group had swept up through the center of the unsuspecting hamlet, knocking off several huts. The VC, swept back by the relentless attack of the command element, finally were able to organize and return effective fire. This was most evident when a flanking fusillade dropped three of the Ping riflemen with them.

One was obviously dead, but the other two rolled in agony in an exposed area between two huts. Malpractice McCorckel took only time to yell over at Archie Dobbs, "Cover me!"

"You got it, pal!" Archie rushed over to one side. He swept the area just beyond the wounded men with shifting volleys of semiautomatic fire, aiming as best he could while concentrating more on volume than accuracy.

Andrea Thuy, who had been close to Malpractice when he took off, didn't hesitate in covering the other flank. She went to a position a scant fifteen meters from Archie. The young Eurasian flipped her M16 onto full automatic and added sweeps of flying slugs that interspersed with the rounds Archie fired into the enemy positions.

Falconi made an attempt to join her, but the only avenue open to Andrea's position was exposed to VC fire. It was to his credit that he tried twice before being forced back to the cover offered by a nearby hut.

Tsang, squatting there with Sparks Martin, grinned widely at the Black Eagles commander. "You no worry, oh-you-kid! Warrior-Sister never die!"

"Yeah," Falconi said peering carefully over at the small segment of the larger battle. "I sure as hell hope not."

"Enemy can no kill Chin-Sza-Tung," Tsang insisted.

Falconi, at that point, knew there was every possibility that the enemy might very well kill "Warrior-Sister." "Maybe she isn't Chin-Sza-Tung," he said. "She never said she was."

"No sweat, oh-you-kid," Tsang said confidently. "That Chin-Sza-Tung."

Sparks, also aware of the possible dire consequences if Andrea became a casualty, shook his head slowly as he glanced at Falconi. "Know any handy prayers, skipper?"

"I'm half Catholic and half Hebrew, but I've never run across any that apply to a fighting goddess from the sky," Falconi said.

Tsang laughed loudly. "Ha! Ha! Christian and Jew think they so civilized, and don't know shit about a Warrior-Sister."

Falconi displayed a weak grin, then looked pointedly over at Andrea who concentrated on the deadly task ahead of her. *Damn you, you beautiful doll, don't get your sweet little ass shot, whatever you do!*

Malpractice, not wasting a beat of time, ran like hell toward the wounded Pings. The air around him zipped and zapped with flying slugs going in all directions, but he kept pounding across the ground toward his objectives. There was no time for a preliminary examination when he reached the wounded men. He simply grabbed each by the collar, then ran like hell back to his starting point, dragging the injured little mercenaries as fast as he could.

Andrea and Archie, now both on full auto, hosed lead from their weapons in a steady stream. Dirt, bark, and splinters flew from the huts the VC used for cover.

One bold Red, anxious to put a bullet into the American rescuing the Chinese mercs, took a chance. He rose up and fired a quick shot at the running Malpractice McCorckel. Not only did he miss, but a round from Andrea's weapon crashed into his skull, exploding his cranium and causing a red-gray splatter of brains and goo to go over the VC's startled comrades.

The two wounded Pings, being hauled across the ground by the intrepid medic, gritted their teeth against the horrible pain and endured the agonies of hell, until Malpractice literally flung them behind the hut where Falconi, Tsang, and Sparks waited.

Falconi shouted quick orders. "Andrea! Archie! Pull back! *Now!*"

Using an unrehearsed but effective method of fire and withdrawal, the pair covered each other in a leap-frogging pattern until they joined the others behind the hut.

Malpractice quickly tended to the wounded men. One injured Ping, his eyes glistening with grateful, loving tears, looked up into Andrea's beautiful face. "*Sheung-Tai po-yau nei!*" he exclaimed gratefully.

Andrea pointed to Malpractice. "He's the one that rescued you. Thank the *wai-shang-tui-ping.*"

"But he did it with your blessings, Chin-Sza-Tung!" the Ping insisted. "So we thank you!"

Falconi, unable to enjoy any displays of good manners at the time, swung his Prick-Six radio off his shoulder. "Alpha. Bravo. This is Falcon. Over." He waited until Top and Kim responded. "The center of the village is secured. Move forward and complete the job. Out."

Tsang, listening nearby, turned to his own troops. "Wait!" He glared at Falconi. "We not do nothing."

Andrea quickly understood that the Ping leader thought Falconi was overriding her authority. "I have already given the orders to continue the assault to *Shiu-Kaau* Falconi. You were not close enough to hear."

Tsang bowed apologetically. "*Ngoh kok-tak ho naan-kwoh*, Chin-Sza-Tung!"

The shooting built up on the flanks, giving a loud indication that both the Alphas and Bravos were sweeping forward in the attack. Periodically there would be the *clump* of Kim's M79 grenade launcher added to the battle's noise.

By now the VC were hard-pressed. The direction of the Black Eagles' attack had been designed to pin the Reds between themselves and an impassible stand of tangled jungle trees and vines.

The plan had worked perfectly, but unfortunately it also had the effect of consolidating the Viet Cong and putting them into a stronger defensive position.

The Black Eagles and Pings formed their own perimeter facing the enemy, either hastily digging in, or occupying abandoned VC positions.

"We make attack!" Tsang insisted. But he looked to Andrea for confirmation.

Using their preconceived signals, Falconi scratched his face to indicate he approved of the idea.

"Yes," Andrea said. "We will use *Sz-kwan-cheung* Kim's special weapon to soften them up first."

115

"As you wish," Falconi said. He gave quick instructions over the small radio to that effect.

Within seconds, the M79 barked quickly a half dozen times. The resulting explosions erupted in the Red positions.

"*Kung kik!*" Tsang screamed, giving the order to attack.

The Pings, completely swept up in the spirit of the assault, gave in to their careless ways. They leaped up and ran wildly toward the Viet Cong.

Return fire burst from the enemy, raking the ranks of the Chinese mercenaries, spilling or violently knocking them to the ground.

"*Gaaung-Po! Gaaung-Po!*" the Pings shouted despite the caualties they took. The living leaped over the bodies of the dead as they pressed forward into the hell of the VC fire.

Archie Dobbs, caught up in the emotions of the moment, winked at Falconi. "What the hell?" He crawled out of his fighting hole and joined the assault, yelling at the top of his lungs. "Airborne! Airborne! All the way!"

"Goddamn it!" Falconi swore angrily. He'd wanted to direct a careful fire-and-maneuver movement through the available cover to close up with the Red guerrillas, but everything had gone to hell at that moment. The situation had collapsed into a do-or-die effort. "As skirmishers!" he yelled to the Black Eagles. "Move out!"

The survivors of the first wave of Pings reached the enemy lines, as the second wave caught up with them. By the time the Black Eagles arrived, there was fierce hand-to-hand fighting.

Andrea Thuy, sticking close to Falconi as he had ordered her to, charged into the contact area with the command element. But a sudden counterattack by a suicidal trio of VC separated her from the others.

116

One of the Reds was hit in the head with a stray round from a distant weapon that might have even belonged to one of his comrades.

Andrea, holding the M16 at waist level, squeezed off two quick shots that slammed into the second VC. He snarled in angry pain as the bullets tore away chunks of his living flesh. His knees went rubbery in an instant, and he collapsed to the ground holding on to his massive wounds.

The young Eurasian woman swung the muzzle toward the third guerrilla who had been behind his friends. He was charging wildly toward her, a long scream of rage bellowing from his open mouth. Andrea pulled the trigger of her rifle.

Nothing happened. Only an ominous click. In the excitement of the battle, she had shot off the last rounds in the magazine.

The Red, a short bayonet on his Chinese-made Soviet M1944 rifle, lunged at her with the deadly blade.

Andrea executed a lightning quick, verticle butt-stroke against the man's weapon, knocking it out of the way. She quickly stepped inside to further block his use of the bayonet. Her next blow was a horizontal swipe with the M16 barrel across the VC's face. The large front sight ripped his cheek open from eye to jawline. He pulled away, swinging back with his own weapon in an instinctive gesture. Luckily for him, he struck the young woman's rifle.

Andrea's M16 spun away under the impact, landing several meters from her.

The Viet Cong grinned now despite his painful facial wound. He lunged at her with the bayonet. Andrea parried the attempt with a *teshio* blow of her hand, then pivoted and delivered a *mde geri keage* kick that connected solidly with the man's jaw.

He screamed again. His mandible, shattered and

useless, hung limply from the smashed joints.

Andrea smashed his exposed adam's apple with a *shuto* chop that forced bloody meat into his windpipe. Now in complete shock, the Viet Cong collapsed with one hand holding his mangled throat while the other was clamped over his broken jaw.

He suffocated quickly in his own blood and mucus.

Andrea retrieved her weapon and turned her attention back to the battle after inserting a fresh magazine.

The fighting was obviously over now, but the Pings were still too excited to control. They fired wildly into the bodies of the dead VC now piled high after their last, desperate stand.

Andrea's voice was shrill above the firing. *"T'ing-foh! T'ing-foh!"* she ordered.

Gradually the Chinese mercs calmed down and obeyed her, stopping the wasteful shooting.

Tsang quickly took command of his men. He formed them up, then on his command, they bowed deeply toward Andrea.

The Ping leader, putting his hands into a prayerful attitude, spoke with a loving tone in his voice to her. *"Toh-tse nei ke pong-choh*, Chin-Sza-Tung."

Andrea nodded her head to him and replied in English. "You are welcome. Now we must return to the village to plan our next operation against the Viet Cong *yau-kik tui.*"

Falconi made a subtle gesture to her, indicating the dead Pings. Andrea caught his meaning. When she spoke again, her voice was angry. "Too many of the Ping-Yan-Uen died in this battle! I told you I did not want this!"

Tsang shuddered and fell to the ground. *"Ngoh kok-tak ho naan-kwott*, Chin-Sza-Tung!"

"To be sorry is not enough!" Andrea said. "I will not have this."

The Ping leader, filled with shame, repeated his

118

apology. "*Ngoh kok-tak ho naan-kwott!* It is so great an honor to die in a battle with Chin-Sza-Tung, that the men cannot help themselves. They are filled with battle lust, which is stronger than what is felt when one needs a woman."

"There are not enough men to allow them to die needlessly," Andrea argued. "Only the Ping-Yan-Uen can produce more Ping-Yan-Uen with their women. Even the sacred generals cannot make soldiers for us."

Falconi turned from them and surveyed the destroyed VC hamlet. The Ping bodies were numerous among the dead Viet Cong. Too numerous. Unless their penchant for irrational fighting was not nipped in the bud immediately, this whole operation could fail. And if the local Red guerrillas ever were reinforced, the chances for a victory here would diminish to a deadly uncertainty.

CHAPTER NINE

The light from the flaming torches danced through the village, shining in flickering brilliance on the bodies of the fourteen Ping-Yan-Uen who had fallen in the battle at the Viet Cong hamlet. They were laid out on crudely fashioned funeral biers, with a pallbearer at each corner of the death-litters.

At one time in the history of this ancient cult of mercenary soldiers, the dead had been sent to their glory with elaborate trappings. The warriors were always dressed in their finest clothing and armor, with favorite weapons strapped to the cadaver. These arms went to the spirit world with their owners, where they could be used by the dead men in celestial battles in which the slain and wounded always quickly recovered at the end of the fighting. Then all—victors and vanquished—gathered to celebrate the joy of the holy combat at a huge feast.

And the men's widows had gone with them, too. Doped to the gills with opium, the women would hurl themselves into the funeral flames to accompany their men into the Ping-Yan-Uen generalship to offer them sensual pleasures to be enjoyed between the sacred battles of the gods.

But things were different now. Modern warfare and

lack of wealth had cut deeply into the old ways.

Weapons could not be sacrificed even for this holy undertaking. Each rifle was an invaluable object that could not be replaced like the swords of old. At one time the Ping-Yan-Uen craftsmen fashioned their people's weapons. But the old swords and spears were no longer of any use in combat. Contemporary fighting called for rifles and machine guns. Unfortunately, without a history or background of up-to-date technology, the Ping-Yan-Uen lacked the modern means to manufacture firearms now. Also, there was no power available to operate the necessary machine shops for such industry, nor the extra parts for necessary repairs and maintenance.

At that moment these modern dead were dressed in their best clothing according to the old customs, but there were no fine silk kimonos or armor fashioned by skilled artisans. Instead, that day's Ping-Yan-Uen dead would report to the afterworld in attire which consisted of faded fatigue uniforms and cheap handmade sandals. Good boots were taken from the dead in a pragmatic effort to keep the living well shod. There was also a change in tradition where their widows were concerned. Women had grown dearer over the years. These people had no replacement centers like modern armies did. Their future fighting strength depended on the birthrate. Thus, with having to keep their population as large as possible, the Pings considered allowing a woman in her childbearing years to kill herself—even to accompany a dead husband to give him sexual gratification in the afterworld—a big waste. After making a proper good-bye to her dead husband, the modern Ping-Yan-Uen either chose, or was assigned, a new husband. Even if she had to share him with another wife. Her job was to serve a man, maintain as permanently a state of pregnancy as possible, and to keep her mouth shut.

Due to the fighting customs of their people, most of the Ping wives were now with their third or fourth husbands.

Falconi, Andrea, Top, and Kim stood together at the head of the funeral procession. Andrea, assumed to be a goddess, stayed off a bit by herself while she dispensed blessings to the Pings who came up to her and knelt at her feet.

"*Chuk nei hang wan*," she spoke softly touching each on the head.

"*Toh-tse*, Chin-Sza-Tung," they mumbled reverently before moving back to their places in the ceremony.

Suddenly loud gongs sounded, and the funeral began.

Pallbearers picked up the portable biers and began a slow march out of the village to the place designated for the ceremonies. Tsang, dressed in his ancient costume for the occasion, led the way while holding the sword above his head. Behind him, striking gongs to mark the cadence of the walk, were other people wearing remnants of the old-style clothing.

Andrea was given a special place between the gong-beaters and the biers. Directly behind her walked Falconi, Top, and Kim as the highest ranking Black Eagles.

Finally, bringing up the rear of the procession came the other Ping soldiers and the Black Eagles. The women and children followed them, but only went as far as the village limits before stopping.

Falconi, glancing around in a subtle manner, noticed a strange thing about this particular funeral. There was a marked lack of grief. There was plenty of somber dignity, no denying that, but nobody seemed particularly sad. He nudged Top Gordon. "Notice the lack of tears?"

Top nodded. "Right, skipper. I suppose since the Pings believe these guys are off to a better world to live as spirits, they're rather happy for them."

"Yeah, I suppose," Falconi said. "And they don't really feel the dead will be gone either. They figure they'll be hovering around as phantom generals to help them out in future battles as a sort of phantom operations section."

"No wonder the little devils aren't afraid to die," Top said.

"That's what's scaring the hell out of me, Top. I'll be glad when this job is over and we're exfiltrated."

"Me too," Top answered. "If this ever developed into an extended campaign, there'd be no getting out of it alive—for anyone."

"I've been worried about Andrea, too," Falconi remarked further. "Even if she keeps denying she's this Warrior-Sister, they insist she is. If something goes wrong, they'll react badly."

"Damn! We could end up fighting the VC *and* the Pings," Top surmised.

"Wouldn't that be lovely?" Falconi asked.

The two lapsed back into silence as the morbid parade marched into a large clearing. The pallbearers carried the biers to designated spots where piles of oil-soaked kindling and fagots had already been arranged.

The Pings formed up into a regular military formation with the Black Eagles off to one side. Andrea was up at the front with Tsang.

There were several long moments of silence. Then the Pings' leader spoke in a singsong dialect using ancient magical words that none present could even understand.

After each long phrase there would be a banging of gongs, then the procedure would be repeated.

Finally Andrea stepped forward. Although she hadn't been briefed in any ceremonial procedures, she played it by ear. The young Eurasian woman imitated a few of Tsang's gestures, then spoke in a voice so loud that it echoed into the tropical sky.

"Tsoi-kin, Ping-Yan-Uen," she said. *"Ngoh kok-tak ho naan-kwott. Chuk nei hang wan, Sheung-tseung!"*

The gongs were sounded again, this time for a full five minutes before lapsing into silence.

Tsang motioned to the dozen torch bearers. They stepped forward and tossed their flaming instruments into the fuel. It lit up immediately, the fire building rapidly until the bodies were all but consumed.

"Tsoi-kin! Tsoi-kin!" the Pings called out, making their final farewells to their comrades. *"Tsoi-kin!"*

Then, leaving only the pallbearers as an honor guard, Tsang led the participants out of the clearing and back down the trail to the village.

Falconi and the Black Eagles were astounded at what they saw on their return.

During the ceremony, the women had put bright-colored decorations up on the huts. Long ribbons and brilliant banners were strung across the hamlet's open square. A bountiful feast was laid out, and the Pings had produced some Vietnamese beer from some hidden storage area.

Tsang looked back at Falconi and smiled. "Now we have party and celebrate the good fortune of our dead soldiers!"

Falconi displayed a weak smile, then looked at Top. "What the hell are we going to do?"

Top sighed. "Our best, skipper. And that's about all that's left."

"I just hope to hell our best proves to be good enough," Falconi remarked. "We've got to simmer these Pings down."

"Yeah," Top said echoing his commander's feelings. "And quickly too!"

Maj. Dnang Quong, accompanied by his adjutant,

Lieutenant Trun, strode rapidly across the concrete landing pad to the Russian MI-4 troop carrier helicopter. This area, north of the border with South Vietnam, was secure enough that it could be lit by outdoor floodlights.

The VC battalion commander looked inside the MI-4 and nodded his approval. "How many men can we put in one of these?"

Trun quickly checked his notes. "A squad of eight to eleven men, comrade major."

"And we shall have ten of these machines at our disposal, hey?"

"*Chac-chan*," Trun replied in the affirmative.

"And the pilots?"

"Czechoslovakians, comrade major," the lieutenant answered.

"Not any of our comrades from the north?"

"These are specially trained assault pilots," Trun explained.

Dnang nodded as he continued to study the interior of the aircraft. After satisfying his curiosity, he turned his attention to the outside of the MI-4. He noted a pod mounted on the front of the fuselage. "*Cai nay la cai gi?*"

Trun smiled. "It is the weapons mount, comrade major. We will be able to use these as gunships. The crews can either install Goryunov machine guns or even air-to-ground rockets."

Dnang smiled in sincere delight. "That should give us plenty of fire support."

"Especially with our air controller teams," Trun added. "And they have spent many hours perfecting their skills with the comrades from Czechoslovakia in calling in helicopters to fire on specific targets."

"Falconi and his bandits will not know what hit them," Dnang said. He put a friendly hand on the young officer's shoulder. "I know how eager you are, Trun. You must have done a lot of reading up on these helicopters. Tell me what you've found out."

Trun flushed with pleasure. "Well, comrade, these aircraft are equipped with a Shvetsov Ash-eighty-two V, eighteen cylinder engines which are designed to be two-row radial types. These particular ones were manufactured by our comrades in China at the Harbin State Factory under license agreements with our generous brothers from the Soviet Union."

"Very interesting, young comrade," Dnang said. "And how fast will these go?"

"The cruising speed is seventy-five knots, with a maximum range of two hundred ten nautical miles, comrade major."

"Thank you for the information, comrade," Dnang said. "That should give us quite a radius in which to operate around our base camp." He checked his watch. "We should try and get some rest. We will be moving into the operational area at first light."

"I am too excited to sleep, comrade major," Trun said.

Dnang laughed. "I must admit that I am too. I feel like a brand new subaltern on his first mission."

"It is the certainty of victory that makes you giddy, comrade major."

"Still, we should at least rest a bit," Dnang said. He turned from the aircraft and strolled back toward the hangar his unit was using as a temporary barracks. "We should be as fresh as possible when we get our hands around Falconi's neck."

Trun only took time to glance back at the choppers, then hurried to catch up with his commanding officer.

Music and laughter permeated the village square as the Ping celebration continued. Heaps of steaming rice were on each of the tables that had been set outside the hut. Two whole hogs had been butchered and barbecued

127

(Ping-Yan-Uen style), and the bottles of beer seemed endless.

A special platform had been erected as a special eating place for Falconi, Andrea, and Tsang. The Falcon, finding the beer delicious, did not want to get too drunk. Yet it would have been considered an insult in the Ping culture for him to drink sparingly. So he consumed as much food as he could possibly hold to keep the alcohol from getting into his bloodstream too fast.

Andrea ate and drank sparingly as she always did. She made polite remarks to Tsang now and then, doing her best to appear godlike without overplaying the role. Andrea had to admit to herself that this game in which she was now engaged grew more and more difficult with each passing day.

Tsang was having a ball.

He laughed and drank heavily, his speech growing slurred as he discussed the day's battle with great gusto. He pointed at Chun Kim and laughed. "Kim take his grenade thrower and shoot. Boom! Boom! Boom! Viet Cong sumbitches get exploded up. Ha! Ha! Good time!" He reached over and nudged Falconi. "Hey! What you think of big battle, huh?"

Falconi shrugged. "I'm happy. Except that Warrior-Sister here became angry because so many men died."

Tsang sobered up a bit. "That right!" He looked over at Andrea, his mood sinking to sadness now. "Oh, Chin-Sza-Tung. *Ngoh kok-tak ho naan-kwott!*"

"Let us not dwell on the situation," Andrea said. "There is no point in any more discussion about the dead soldiers."

Falconi groaned inwardly. He most certainly did want to continue the discussion. But there was no way he could do it without making Andrea appear subordinated to him.

Tsang looked in drunken brotherly love at the young

128

woman. "Do you pardon me, then, Chin-Sza-Tung?"

"Yes," Andrea replied.

"Toh-tse, toh-tse!"

Falconi decided to change the subject. "There were many brave deeds performed today."

Tsang became happily excited again. "Yes! Yes!" He leaped to his feet. "Where is the *wai-shang-tui-ping*—the medic? What is his name? Mawprak-ass?"

Falconi laughed. "He is called Malpractice. Do you wish to speak with him?"

"Oh, yes! He a brave man. Risk life to save two Ping-Yan-Uen. You call him here please?"

Falconi waved down at the table where Malpractice sat with Archie Dobbs and Sparks Martin. As soon as the medic noticed he was wanted, he got to his feet and hurried up to the place of honor. He saluted properly. "What's up, skipper?"

"Tsang wants to talk to you," Falconi said.

Tsang stood up unsteadily. "I talk to ever'body." He clapped his hands loudly until the area grew silent. When the Ping's leader finally had everyone's attention, he pointed to Malpractice. "This brave man. Save two men from death in battle today. That make Chin-Sza-Tung happy."

Andrea nodded. "Yes. That made me very happy."

"So now we reward medic," Tsang said. He clapped his hands and pointed over to the women's table. Two of the young Ping-Yan-Uen ladies left their food and scurried over to their people's leader. Tsang leered at them as he spoke. *"Nei nui-yan wai-shang-tui-ping."*

The two Ping women giggled modestly behind their hands.

"What's goin' on?" Malpractice asked.

"We reward you for save two Ping-Yan-Uen soldiers," Tsang said. "These two lose husbands in fight today. They your womans now."

Malpractice's mouth fell open.

"Sure! Sure! *Hui!*" Tsang said laughing. "You make fuck with them."

Malpractice was stunned. "Uh, yeah, but—"

"It would be bad manners to refuse," Falconi said.

"Well, I've always considered the social graces to be of utmost importance," the medic said. Before he could make any further remarks, the two women each grabbed one of his hands and pulled him away to the loud cheers of the crowd. Malpractice started to protest, then displayed a silly grin as he allowed himself to be led from the party to a hut out in the darkness near the jungle.

Archie Dobbs, indignant as hell, leaped to his feet as Malpractice disappeared from the festivities. "That sonofabitch! He tells me I can't get no pussy around here, and he runs off with two of 'em!"

Top Gordon, at another table, guffawed. "See what clean living gets you, Archie?"

"Oh, God," Archie moaned, sitting back down and cradling his face in his hands. "Why the hell wasn't I borned a medic?"

The delivery driver pulled the last bag of dry cleaning from the back of his truck and walked up to the guard in front of the Bachelor Officers Quarters of the South Vietnamese military police garrison that was situated between Peterson Field and Saigon.

The driver nodded respectfully to the sentry. "*Chao Oog, nguoi linh.*"

The soldier, who knew the man from hundreds of similar occasions, raised his hand in a friendly manner. "*Chao ong.* You are working late, *khong*?"

The driver indicated the sign on the side of his truck which proclaimed the vehicle to be from Tan Son Nhut Air Base Dry Cleaning Plant. "We are the most popular

130

establishment in the city. Thus, we are blessed with many clients." Out of habit he showed his ID card.

The guard didn't bother to check the document. He had seen it many times and knew for a fact that it was authentic. "Who are you making the delivery to?"

Trung Uy Trang Loc."

The sentry checked his quarters roster. "Room Twelve."

"*Cam on ong,*" the deliveryman said. He went up the steps and walked down the hallway until he reached the proper door. He knocked rapidly. "*Trung Uy* Trang? Dry cleaning."

The portal was abruptly thrown open and a young officer wearing the uniform of a South Vietnamese lieutenant stood swaying in the entrance. His uniform shirt was unbuttoned and hanging outside his trousers. "Eh? Dry cleaning? Bring it in, *mau lin!*"

The driver scurried into the room noticing the officer was extremely drunk. He smiled as he hung the package in the closet. "Celebrating, hey?"

Trang laughed sardonically. "Celebrating? *Co!* I am happily toasting the fact that I shall never be promoted."

"*Ong noi gi?*"

"Are you deaf? I said I shall never go higher in rank than I am at this very moment." He patted his shoulder boards. "I am doomed to be a lieutenant all my days."

The driver made a condescending gesture. "Surely not! I am certain a young man with your ambition—"

"*Ong hieu khong?* Ambition has nothing to do with it! I could be the most brilliant commander and staff officer in the world, yet I would never be able to advance beyond my present humble place in the army. Do you know why, driver?"

The dry cleaning man shrugged. "*Toi tiec.*"

"Because my family has no influence nor money to pay bribes," Trang said. "I was passed over in favor of a

131

young upstart second lieutenant who was made captain today. His father is a rich merchant from Vung Tau. The old man paid the brigade commander to advance his son over me. And to cause the unbearable to be unendurable, the puppy has become my company commander."

"You sound as if you are a bitter man," the driver said.

The officer grabbed the deliveryman by the collar. He stared into his face. "You impertinent swine! Consider yourself lucky I don't break your face." Then he relaxed and pushed the man away. "*Xin loi ong*. I can't blame you." He staggered across the room and took another drink out of the bottle of scotch on the table by his bed. He whirled and snarled, "But the day will come, my friend, when I find a way to have my revenge on this system which denies a hardworking, loyal officer a decent chance to get ahead."

Rather than being upset by the manhandling he had just endured, the driver seemed pleased. "Perhaps I can help you in your efforts, *Trung Uy*."

The officer laughed. "You? What can a truck driver do to help me get promoted?"

"Nothing to advance your rank," the dry cleaning man said. "But much if you want revenge." Then he abruptly turned and left the room.

The deliveryman went back to his truck and drove from the garrison. He traveled straight into downtown Saigon, turning off into the Cholon District. After leaning on his horn and forcing his vehicle through the streets teeming with people, he wheeled into a back alley and stopped.

As he stepped from the truck, two burly men wordlessly appeared and stationed themselves between it and the entrance to the back street.

The driver walked down some rickety stairs and stepped into a small basement room. A man sitting there

132

leaped to his feet and saluted. "*Co*, Comrade Major Xong?"

"We must send a message to Hanoi," the driver Xong said. "Tonight I have found a turncoat to replace the late Colonel Ngai."

"Yes, comrade major," the other said with a smile. "That will please our superiors very much."

"Indeed," Xong agreed. "Especially when they find this man works in the military police company that provides the security for MAC V headquarters at Peterson Field."

The man's mouth opened. "You mean—"

"Yes! We have another inroad into the Black Eagle organization!" Xong went to a desk and got a pencil and paper. "Warm up the radio. I want this message transmitted tonight."

Capt. Brohumir Sprosty coordinated the movements of his feet and hands that controlled the MI-4 helicopter's flight while he put the aircraft into a steep turn.

As he approached the landing area in the Viet Cong camp, he leaned forward and took a practice aim through the sighting device which controlled the machine guns mounted under the chopper.

Sprosty grinned to himself. He wished the camp was a target. If it were, he could have fired the four barrels of the quad 7.72 millimeter guns and flattened the place like a windstorm had hit it.

This pilot was a Czechoslovakian officer on loan to the North Vietnamese. If that wasn't international enough, he was flying a Russian-type aircraft manufactured in Red China that was on loan to the Viet Cong.

Bohumir Sprosty felt very, very fierce and brave at that moment. After several years of participating in

133

various Warsaw Pact maneuvers, he now had a chance to go into real combat.

He pulled away from the gunsight and settled the aircraft down into the area designated by the ground crewman who was signalling him in. As soon as the tires hit solid earth, Sprosty cut the main rotor, and the helicopter settled down onto its shock absorber system.

Sprosty could feel the aircraft shake as the men inside quickly disembarked. As soon as he freed himself from the seatbelt, he joined them outside. The ground crewmen, well trained, quickly tied the chopper down to the Czech officer's satisfaction. Then he looked skyward at the other nine MI-4s approaching in a trail formation. He turned his attention to a quick inspection of the outside areas of his machine.

Sprosty smiled in anticipation as he treated himself to a look at the machine guns under the nacelle. He couldn't wait to be flying at treetop level, the weaponry spitting death at the men he'd been sent to help destroy.

"Comrade pilot?"

Sprosty turned. "Yes?"

"I am Lieutenant Trun, the adjutant. My commander has requested you to join him at headquarters immediately."

"Of course," Sprosty said politely. "He sounds like a man in a hurry."

"He is, comrade," Trun assured him. "We have every reason to believe we shall be attacked here by the Black Eagles within twenty-four hours. Comrade Major Dnang wants the helicopters ready for action."

"They already are," Sprosty assured him. "All that is necessary to do is to load the machine guns and rocket launchers."

"Excellent, comrade pilot," Trun said enthusiastically. "Then it is of the utmost importance to coordinate

134

our battle plans with your men and the air strike control team."

Sprosty smiled, taking another glance back at his aircraft. The four Goryunov machine gun barrels looked lethal in their pod under the fuselage. He turned back and hurried after the little Vietnamese officer, the thrill of combat already building up in his soul at even this early hour.

CHAPTER TEN

There was hardly a sound as the Black Eagles and their Ping comrades-in-arms moved through the dew-slicked vegetation of the early morning jungle.

Archie Dobbs had completed a long and detailed reconnaissance on the target sight less than a quarter of an hour previously. The Black Eagles scout's report had been encouraging. The objective, the final Viet Cong village in the operational area, appeared to be quiet and nearly deserted. Only a few, lightly armed guerrillas could be discerned either sleeping or standing an exhausted tour of sentry duty.

"They sure as hell ain't expectin' nothin', skipper," Archie had told his commander.

"After the previous engagement they probably figure we'd whipped them as bad as we wanted to," Falconi answered. "No doubt their CO is banking on being left alone for awhile."

Archie had grinned viciously. "Yeah? Well, he fucked up, didn't he?"

Falconi had winked at his scout. "A safe assumption, young soldier."

Now, strung out in three separate lines of conflicts, the temporary allied army of Falconi's men and the Ping-

Yan-Uen continued their careful approach to the objective.

Top Gordon's Alphas occupied the center of the first rank. There was a squad of Pings on each of their flanks. Behind them, organized in the same manner, came Kim's Bravos. The Korean marine had his M16 slung over his shoulder. He carried his beloved M79 grenade launcher with extra ammo pouches clipped onto his belt. Falconi, Tsang, Andrea Thuy, and the command element brought up the rear. This was the best place from which to direct a battle that was conceived to be a turkey shoot. The affair wasn't expected to last much more than fifteen minutes.

Top's voice came over the Falcon's radio. "This is Alpha. We're coming out of the jungle now. Contact with unfriendlies imminent. Out."

Within five seconds there was a burst of firing. Kim's launcher barked, and the battle was on.

The initial advance into the hamlet was easy. The Viet Cong's defense was weak and half-hearted. They fired a few rounds at the attackers, then quickly fled into the interior of their tiny jungle town.

"Gaaung-Po!"

The Pings ran forward without regard to covering each other or directing their fire at specific targets.

Kim's Bravos and their own Chinese mercs next hit the village. They had to pick up the pace in order to maintain contact with the Alphas. Kim exchanged his launcher for the M16. With the combat formation broken up, there was no way he could safely determine where to fire the grenades. There was a good chance they might land in the middle of Top's men if they had advanced farther than expected.

Falconi and his group swept in from the jungle at a dead run. Archie Dobbs, as undisciplined as the Pings, sped off to catch up with the fighting.

Several of the thatched huts had caught fire from

138

tracer rounds, and a dense cloud of smoke began to pour from the wet structures. The firing died down to an occasional shot, and in moments it was easy to hear men's voices shouting to each other in the early morning gloom.

Falconi looked over at Andrea. "A piece of cake."

"This will wrap it up," she whispered moving close to him. "And I'm glad! Being a goddess is a bit demanding."

"I can certainly believe that," Falconi said.

She smiled at him. "But I'll admit I'm going to miss being worshiped."

"I knew the job was going to your head," Falconi remarked, grinning back at her. "But get ready to come down off your high horse. We should be exfiltrated the hell out of here within twenty-four hours."

The firing stopped. A peaceful stillness filled the heavy atmosphere of the early morning.

Falconi spoke into his radio. "Team leaders, report. Over."

"Alpha objective secured. No more resistance. Out," Top said.

"Same-same us Bravos. Out," Kim reported in.

Tsang joined the Falcon and Andrea. His face showed his disappointment. "Not much fight. Too bad." Then he glanced at Andrea and smiled. "But nobody killed. You happy, Chin-Sza-Tung?"

"Yes. I am very pleased."

Archie's voice came over the radio. "This is the scout. Tell the cook to turn the pancakes—over."

Falconi barked into his own radio, "Knock it off, Archie!"

"Roger, skipper."

The Black Eagles' commander shook his head. "That guy's humor surfaces at the damnedest times."

Malpractice McCorckel had heard the exchange. "Ten thousand comedians outta work, and Archie's tryin' to

139

be funny."

Sparks Jackson, glad to have left the larger radio back in the Ping village, was in a good mood. "What the hell? Let's lighten up, guys. Things are goin' okay right now, ain't they?"

"Yeah," Falconi replied. "When we get back we can tell MAC V to start the big move into here."

Everyone felt good. It had been a great operation. They had taken no casualties, and Operation Guerrilla Hell was now wrapped up tight in a bright, red ribbon, and ready to be tucked away under Chuck Fagin's Christmas tree. The only thing left to do was to search the area thoroughly for any hardware or documents that might prove interesting to intelligence back in Saigon.

Then the shit hit the fan.

Heavy rifle fire poured out of the surrounding jungle into their ranks. This attack was U shaped and almost had the Black Eagles and Pings outflanked. Within seconds, heavy automatic weapons joined in to support the enemy riflemen.

"Alpha! Bravo! Withdraw!" Falconi shouted into his radio.

The outfit formed up in the hellish confusion and returned fire. It was pitifully weak in comparison to the amount they were receiving.

"Alpha, this is Falcon. Over."

"This is Alpha. Over," came Top's reply.

"Give me a quick guesstimate on what the hell's going on. Over," Falconi ordered.

"We walked into this one," Top reported, his voice distorted by both the firing and the radio. "There's a force of two to three hundred bad guys to our front and flanks. Plenty of automatic weapon support. I'm in the process of hauling ass. Out."

"Roger," Falcon acknowledged. "Bravo, what's your situation? Over."

Kim's voice was excited. "Plenty of big trouble, Falcon. Taking lots of fire. Over."

"How many VC do you figure is in your area? Over," Falconi asked.

"There are more VC than stars in night sky. Over." Kim replied.

Falconi looked at Malpractice. "That's all I need right now—an Oriental philosopher speaking in his culture's abstract terminology." He spoke again in the radio. "Bravo, give me a more definite number. Over."

Kim spoke again. "More VC than waves in ocean. Over."

"Christ!" Falconi swore. "I've got to get a definite count." He tried again. "Are there any of the American guys near you? If so, give 'em the radio. Over."

A moment later, Blue Richards's voice came over the air. "This is Bravo. Over."

Thank God, a good ol' no-nonsense country boy that knows how to count, Falconi's mind spoke to him. "How many Viet Cong are you up against over there? Over."

Blue answered, "A whole shit-pot full. Over."

"*Oh, goddamn it!*" Falconi bellowed in rage. He knew he'd simply have to make his own guess about what they were facing. He turned and motioned to Archie, Sparks, and Malpractice. "We've got a battalion or so going up against us. The Alphas and Bravos are going to be moving back through here. So let's get ready to give 'em covering fire when we link up."

Andrea Thuy and Tsang joined the hastily formed defensive line. For a full five minutes they could do nothing but wait until the battle rolled back their way.

Then the first combatants made their appearance.

This was Kim's Bravos and their Pings. They backed into the area, shooting occasionally but unable to lay down any effective fire for fear of hitting the Alphas.

"Kim!" Falconi yelled to the Korean marine. "Put

your guys in with us and stand fast. When the Alphas get here they're going to have a few hundred bad guys right on their asses. They're going to need help."

"Roger, skipper!" Kim acknowledged. He quickly situated his people and had time to personally check their fields of fire before the other segment of combat, under great pressure, stumbled back to join them.

Calvin Culpepper, Toby Barker, and a few Pings were the first to appear. From their actions, it was easy to determine that Top was running a fire-and-withdrawal maneuver in which one group of his guys kept the VC at bay with sustained firing while the others retreated to safer positions before throwing out supporting fire. This would then allow the first bunch to run like hell for a more secure area.

Calvin, Toby, and their buddies flung themselves down and picked zones of fire to cover. Within scant seconds, the remainder of the Alphas appeared running like hell. Top brought up the rear, and as soon as he joined the main body, Falconi gave him his orders.

"Gather up your guys and withdraw about twenty or twenty-five meters. As soon as you're in position to give us supporting fire, let me know."

"Right, skipper." Top quickly pulled the Alphas and their Pings out of the perimeter and moved out to follow the battle instructions.

Falconi's voice sounded loud in the sudden quiet. "Get ready! They'll hit us hard as hell in just a—"

Hundreds of Soviet-bloc small arms exploded ahead of them. Dirt, dead leaves, twigs, splinters from trees, and other debris filled the air. Ricochets sung off into nothing while stray rounds zipped overhead like angry hornets. The noise of the shooting was a deafening, unending roar of thunder.

The defensive line, with picked men on full automatic, fired back a weaker volume of spitting ammo than they

142

were receiving, but the first rank of VC were bunched up and careless. The flying slugs smacked into the charging Commies. They bucked and whirled under the impact of the slugs, falling into writhing, bloody piles of bullet-butchered meat.

Top's voice came over the Prick-Six. "Falcon, this is Alpha. In position. Out."

The Red guerrillas farther behind caught up and were now colliding with their own dead. They grew cautious and held up. This was exactly what Falconi was waiting for.

"Bug out!" he yelled.

Everyone leaped to their feet and cut loose with rapid, unaimed firing, then turned and ran as fast as they could rearward. They continued across the Bravos' positions and kept going for another twenty-five meters before Falconi ordered a halt.

Once again they took up defensive positions.

Falconi had just situated himself when he felt a vicious kick to his left ankle. Infuriated he looked up to see Tsang. Falconi grabbed the mercenary's leg and pulled him down. "What's the big idea?"

Tsang's face was distorted with rage. "You no let Chin-Sza-Tung run battle."

"Shut the fuck up!" Falconi yelled. "She told me to take over, you sonofabitch!"

"Hey, you the sumbitch, goddamn it!" Tsang shrieked.

Andrea, nearby, quickly crawled over. She grabbed Tsang's sleeve and shook him hard. "*T'ing-po!* You do what *Shiu-Kaau* Falconi tells you!"

"But you are Chin-Sza-Tung the Warrior-Sister!" Tsang protested.

"*Tsing ti!* Follow orders!"

"Yes, Chin-Sza-Tung," Tsang said. "*Ngoh kok-tak ho naan-kwoh.*"

"Don't make me angry again!" Andrea hissed.

143

"I obey," Tsang said.

Falconi quickly forgot the encounter. "Malpractice! Sparks! I'm shifting you to the Alphas. Join 'em when they come running through here."

"Roger, Falcon!"

"Aye, aye, sir!"

Falconi glared at Tsang. "Pick a half dozen of your men to go, too!"

Tsang looked first to Andrea, then he nodded and crawled off to attend to the chore.

The shooting, which had subsided somewhat, quickly built back into a screaming roar. Then Top and his men appeared, running like hell, from the front. As they rushed back to take up new positions, Malpractice and Sparks leaped up to join them. The six Pings chosen by Tsang to accompany the Bravos were close on their heels as they streaked through the jungle.

Falconi and his group again threw out a hailstorm of fire. The first VCs, anxious but unfortunate, stumbled into the initial swarm of 5.56 slugs, toppling to the ground. The Reds behind them, perceiving that once more they had come upon a waiting line of resistance, went to the cover afforded by the vegetation to advance at a slower pace.

"Haul ass!" Falconi yelled.

Everyone leaped up and fired before renewing the withdrawal effort. Toby Barker, however, was not so lucky. He got to his feet and hosed out a stream of slugs, then turned to run for the rear. But he failed to see a large root in the obscured path he was following and tripped over it. The marine went down and rolled once. He was back on his feet in one quick move.

But it was enough of a delay to allow the leading elements of the VC to catch up with him.

Seven point sixty-two millimeter Chinese bullets sung a buzzing death melody around him. Toby turned back

144

toward the enemy. He caught sight of the nearest. "Semper Fi, motherfucker!"

Toby's fireburst of six rounds scored hundred percent, the impact hurling the small Viet Cong into a flailing cartwheel.

But a determined Red cut loose with his AK47 from a distance of only ten meters.

Toby felt the blows of the slugs. He staggered back under the powerful pounding but managed to fire again. The man who had shot him suddenly dropped his weapon as his chest was ripped apart by Toby's bullets.

But it was too late.

The marine sat down, feeling weak. He tried to get up, then noticed the black pajama-clad Red in front of him. Toby flipped the sonofabitch the bird, then rolled over and died.

The guerrilla, an old vet of the Viet Minh, didn't quite understand the gesture—but he admired it. "Too bad, G.I. Joe," he said. Without pausing, he rushed off to join his unit's rolling attack.

Falconi's tactics finally paid off. After a two-hour running battle, they managed to break contact with the overwhelming force of Viet Cong.

The Black Eagles and Pings crossed a shallow jungle valley and set up positions on the far side. Everyone was exhausted. A quick check showed that eight Pings were lost—and Sgt. Toby Barker.

Andrea took advantage of the situation to speak with Tsang. "We must listen to Falconi," she told the Ping leader.

"Why?" Tsang asked. "You are Chin-Sza-Tung. The legends say you will lead us."

"I do not think I am your Warrior-Sister," Andrea said. "Yet let me say this to you. If I am Chin-Sza-Tung,

145

and I feel that *Shiu-Kaau* Falconi is a great commander, then it must be so. Or perhaps the old generals wish for us to follow him."

"If he is a great commander, why did we have no victory today?"

"We were surprised by a force we didn't know was there," Andrea said. "Yet, despite their outnumbering us by a great deal, they did not defeat us."

Tsang shook his head and rubbed his eyes. "There is much to ponder here."

"Pray to the generals," Andrea said.

"Yes! I must pray to the generals."

Archie Dobbs interrupted them. "The Falcon wants you two over with the team leaders. He's going to have a conference of war."

Andrea nodded. "Yes. Thank you."

"It should be your conference, Chin-Sza-Tung," Tsang said. "Our legend is emphatic. It is *you* who will lead us to the throne of China. Not a *Mei-Kwok*."

"Never mind. We must obey the Falcon."

The two left their position and joined Falconi, Top Gordon, and Chun Kim. The Black Eagle commander wasted no time. "We've been set up."

"And how!" Top agreed. "We walked into that one. The original VC outfit has been tripled or quadrupled since the last firefight."

"There's no doubt we've got a battalion-sized unit going against us here," Falconi said. "We'll have to call in reinforcements."

Kim took advantage of the lull to clean his M79 grenade launcher. "We need men and heavy weapons," he said. "VC got big stuff."

"Yeah," Falconi said. "When we get back to the Ping village, we'll radio in a report. I imagine they'll pull us out of here and bring in a major line unit to slug it out with these new Viet Cong."

146

"You sure they new boys?" Kim asked.

"No doubt," Falconi said. "Like Top said, they weren't in this area when we first arrived."

"Maybe they were sent in to take us on," Top suggested.

"I don't know," Falconi said with a tone of uncertainty in his voice. "It could be just a coincidence. If our brass suddenly decided this area was important enough for a big buildup, then the Commie higher-ups could do the same."

Tsang offered some information. "This is first time big VC outfit in here, I tell you that. It is strange game the fates—or the generals—play with us."

"It'll be out of our hands soon," Falconi said. "From here on, we'll have to be careful, but I don't see any problem in getting back to the village."

"When we get there, I pray to generals for guidance," Tsang said. "I confused, not sure no more. Very bad."

"Good idea," Falconi said. Then he knew there was something he had to do, in order to smooth things over between himself and Tsang. "I was impolite to you and raised my voice in stupid anger during the fighting. I apologize."

Tsang nodded his acceptance, his embarrassment canceled out by this polite, face-saving gesture on the American's part. "That good. No sweat, oh-you-kid. Chin-Sza-Tung tell me to keep cool head."

Andrea smiled. "Everything will be all right, I'm sure."

Falconi started to speak again but stopped. He listened for several moments. "What the hell is that?"

"What?" Top asked.

"I not hear something," Kim said.

"Listen!" Falconi admonished them.

Tsang shrugged. "There no—"

"Shhhh!"

147

The sound grew gradually louder until the undeniable chop-chop of helicopter engines could be easily heard.

Falconi looked at Sparks. "We didn't call in any aircraft, did we?"

"No, skipper."

"There they are!" Top said.

The shapes of low-flying choppers could be discerned through the treetops. Suddenly Falconi exclaimed, "Oh, shit!"

"What matter, oh-you-kid?" Tsang asked.

"Those are Russian MI-4s!"

"With weapons pods," Top added ominously. "Wonder where they're flying to?"

Archie Dobbs, sitting nearby, was never disoriented no matter how thick the jungle. "Can't you tell? That's a direct course back to the Ping village."

Captain Sprosty banked the MI-4 helicopter and swept down toward the settlement. He grinned to himself as he spotted the people rushing from the huts to look upward at his slow sixty-knot approach.

"Not expecting aircraft from the north, eh?" he said. "Well, you running dogs of the American gangsters, this war has taken a new turn."

He pushed down on the collective control allowing his machine to lower itself. When he was a few meters above treetop level, Sprosty spoke to his companion chopper which hovered close by. "*Dobry den*, young Lieutenant Somad. *Jak se mate?*"

The other, a young subaltern, quickly answered. "I am fine, *dekuji*, Captain Sprosty."

"Are you ready to attack?" Sprosty asked him.

"*Ano!* Yes!"

"Follow me in," Sprosty ordered. He pushed forward on the cyclic control, and the helicopter moved ahead.

The speed increased with the turn of the throttle. When he reached a point a hundred meters from the village, Sprosty squeezed the trigger mounted on the stick.

The quartet of Goryunov machine guns in the weapons pod kicked to life, spurting streams of 7.62 millimeter slugs into the inhabitants who stood in several groups around the hamlet's square. Dirt flew up as the screaming fusillade cut a path through the hapless people who collapsed under the crush of the four coordinated volleys the chopper's firing system contained.

After passing over the jungle town, Sprosty turned away, swinging his aircraft around so he could look back at the destruction he had just dealt his civilian targets.

Lieutenant Somad spoke excitedly over the radio. *"Dobra, kapitan!* You have scored many hits!"

Sprosty picked up his microphone. *"Dobre*, Lieutenant Somad. Now give them the rockets!"

"Ano, kapitan," Somad replied. Then he dove to the attack, the rockets mounted on the sides of his fuselage now streaking groundward into the human carnage below.

CHAPTER ELEVEN

Lt. Trang Loc stood in front of the platoon he commanded in the Special Military Police Company. The highly disciplined, handpicked troops were aligned in unwavering ranks, the sun glistening off their helmet liners. Trang's impassive face was a mask that covered a seething rage and hatred that boiled in the depths of his soul.

The other three platoons were also drawn up smartly in front of the unit orderly room. Trang glanced at the other subalterns, then reluctantly swung his eyes over to look at the company commander who stood at the front of the outfit. This captain was a twenty-year-old upstart who had been promoted through the bribes and influence of his father. Trang, on the other hand, had entered the army as an enlisted man. His long years of service began in the old colonial army during the fight against the Viet Minh. Those days had been fraught with combat and hard work as he attained the necessary qualification for entrance into the Republic of Vietnam's Officer Academy. When he'd finally been admitted as a cadet, Trang was a tried-and-true sergeant, ready to take on the extra responsibilities and leadership of higher rank, rank in his country's struggle against Communist aggression. Until recently he was slated for promotion to captain and the assignment as the commander of the company.

But money and favors had exchanged hands between a punk second lieutenant's wealthy family and officers in the adjutant general's department as well as the brigade commander. The result of this double-dealing, was Trang's being passed over in the search for a new captain. Thus, his much deserved promotion went to the kid who now barked orders in his falsetto voice.

"Platoon leaders," the new captain called out, "take charge of your units and take them to their duty stations."

Trang slowly raised his hand in an insincere salute, then did an about-face. He barked a few orders in his crisp, efficient way, and his platoon of elite guards swung out in step. He marched them out of the military police compound and over to MAC V Headquarters only a few meters away.

The sentries at the gate snappily presented arms as this group of special MPs marched in. Trang halted them and turned the small detachment over to the platoon sergeant. Then he went inside the building to report to his own post in the communications section. This area was so sensitive that it was thought best that the highest ranking member of the ARVN guard use it as his command post.

When Trang entered this super secret part of the building, he wasted no time in reporting to his own office where, as officer of the guard, he personally supervised the security of the building. Trang found the American CIA agent Chuck Fagin sitting on his desk. Fagin nodded a greeting and stood up. "I hope you don't mind my waiting around here."

"No, Mr. Fagin," Trang replied in perfect but accented English. "Something special going on?"

"Yeah. I'm waiting for some urgent messages that

are overdue."

Trang took off his helmet liner and sat it on the desk. "I imagine that concerns your favorite group—the Black Eagles."

"As always," Fagin answered.

"I trust Major Falconi is not in some difficulty."

"He may well be," Fagin said. "His routine commo check is late."

"The major is a real ass-kicker," Trang said. "That's probably what he is doing this very minute." He laughed. "If Falconi had the choice of killing the enemy or talking on the radio—he would be shooting."

"Perhaps—" Fagin was interrupted by the arrival of the chief of communications. This man, also from the CIA, was short, bald, and perspiring heavily despite the air conditioning. Fagin eyed him closely. "I don't like the expression on your face, Fred."

"Sorry if I'm showing too much concern," Fred Cayman apologized, "but we haven't gotten as much as a buzz out of Falcon."

"How long has it been?" Fagin inquired.

Cayman had the latest commo log. He flipped open the pages. "It's been thirty-six hours since the last regular contact," he said after perusing the document, "and we've been trying to raise 'em for the past twelve hours on a regular basis."

"How regular?"

"Every fifteen minutes," Cayman said. "That adds up to forty-eight unanswered broadcasts."

"Goddamn it!"

"I would think it an accurate assumption that the Black Eagles are in a hairy spot," Cayman said.

Trang went to the map behind him. "They are in Operational Area Bravo, are they not?"

"Right," Fagin answered.

Trang emitted a long, low whistle. "It's a dangerous

153

location, but there's not been much activity there as of late."

"Perhaps that's all changed," Fagin said.

"From the obvious lack of commo contact, I'd venture an unpopular opinion," Cayman said. "It appears as if the Black Eagle Detachment is in deep shit."

"And, if I know Falconi and his boys, they'll be sinking in even deeper," Trang said.

Loud moaning and shrieking greeted the Black Eagles and Pings when they stepped from the jungle into the village. The women, crying hysterically, demonstrated their anguish by throwing themselves on the ground and beating the dirt with their tiny fists.

"*Fei-kei king-kik!*" one screamed.

Tsang turned to Falconi. "She say aircraft attack."

"That's easy to tell," Falconi said in a low tone.

Although the wounded were in the hospital hut, and the dead from the helicopter assault had been picked up and taken to the proper place for the cremation ceremony, the damaged structures and blood-soaked sections of ground still gave stark evidence of the ferocity of the airborne raid.

Casualties would have been heavier, but even the Ping-Yan-Uen women and children were well trained in combat. The first pass of the Red choppers had caught them unawares, but by the time the Czech pilots had turned around for further attacks, the population had headed for the jungle. The wounded had been taken to cover also, leaving only cadavers to absorb more of the machine gun bullets and rocket explosions.

Now, with the fighting men back, the noncombatants ran to them to find out what had brought about the man-made hell that descended on them from the skies.

Tsang, their leader, was absolutely raging. "*Kong*

154

maan ti! I don't understand. If we are receiving divine guidance through Chin-Sza-Tung, why has this terrible thing happened to us?"

Falconi took hold of Andrea's arm. He whispered urgently to her. "Be careful. We've reached a real sensitive area here."

"I'll do my best," Andrea said under her breath. "Let me listen to him for a few moments. Perhaps some of the things the Oriental psychologist told me before the mission may help."

"It had better," Falconi warned her. "We could find ourselves looking down the barrels of Ping weapons."

Sparks Martin, who had gone to his radio to broadcast a report back to MAC V Headquarters, hurried up to Falconi. "I got bad news, skipper. That AN/PRC-forty-one radio is scattered over half the village. And that includes all the spare parts, too. Looks like a close hit from a rocket blew the hell out of our commo."

Falconi gritted his teeth. "Damn! We've got to get some more people and heavier weapons in here. We can't fight helicopters with M16s."

"Especially when they're able to shoot machine guns and rockets at us," Sparks said.

"We have to deal with the Pings first," Falconi told him. "As soon as that problem is settled, we'll turn to whatever else we have to do."

His concern about the tactical side of the operation was interrupted by Tsang. The Ping captain went to the badly shot-up main hut and walked up the steps to the porch. He turned to face his people who had gathered around him.

Tsang took a few moments to survey the damaged village and the troubled expressions on the faces of his people. "It would seem that our *chung-kaau* has brought us to a crisis. There are many questions that must be studied to make sure we are following the right road. I

155

shall make a formal prayer to the *Tseung* and see what they tell me."

As he spoke to his people, the Black Eagles became aware that they were being subtly, but persistently pressed in toward the center of the throng. Archie Dobbs, a man given to claustrophobia, started to get nervous. "I don't like being closed in," he said aloud to no one in particular.

"Easy, Archie," Top said. "We got to play this baby by ear. Overreacting could be a real disaster."

"It may be anyhow," Archie said.

Ray Swift Elk and Calvin Culpepper were shoulder to shoulder as the milling Ping-Yan-Uen kept jostling the group. Swift Elk winked at Calvin. "How you doin', Buffalo Soljer?"

"I'm having a helluva good time, Injun," Calvin said. "I just fought my way out of a damn jungle, and it looks like I might have to do the same right here."

"Everybody cool it," Falconi said. "They're not making any overt moves against us."

"They won't have to, skipper," Archie said. "All they gotta do is start shootin'. We wouldn't stand a chance."

There was a sudden movement of disturbance toward the front of the crowd.

"Christ!" Malpractice said. "They got Andrea!"

They looked up to where Tsang stood on the porch. Within seconds Andrea, held tightly by a pair of husky Pings, was hustled up the steps to him.

Tsang signaled for quiet. "I will ask the *Tseung* about Chin-Sza-Tung," he said. "In a few hours we shall know exactly what we must do."

Falconi noted that Andrea was disarmed and unable to move. He took a quick look around. If any of the Black Eagles so much as displayed a threatening attitude, or even a dirty look, the Pings could shoot all of them down in a matter of only a few seconds.

Robert Mikhailovich Falconi had never felt so helpless in his life.

The tropical evening was fading fast as Lt. Trang Loc returned to the military police garrison from Peterson Field. He watched as his platoon sergeant took the men over to the barracks to dismiss them from their day's duty. He glanced toward company headquarters, knowing that the pip-squeak who was now his commanding officer would not be there. The little bastard had probably been away for hours. He was no doubt with a mistress or sitting in some swank officers' club drinking with his new American friends in celebration of his promotion.

Trang crossed the small barracks yard in angry strides as he went into the officers' quarters. He walked directly down the hall to his room. Once inside, he wasted no time in pouring himself a stiff drink from the bottle of scotch he kept there.

The booze burned his throat. He couldn't afford the better brands and had to content himself with the cheapest of alcoholic drinks. When an officer in the Army of the Republic of Vietnam was forced to live only on his military pay, he hadn't anything left over for the luxuries of life.

There was a knock on the door.

"Yes?" he called out.

"Dry cleaning."

Trang frowned in puzzlement. He looked in his closet and saw that all his uniforms were there. "You have the wrong room."

"Is this not the quarters of *Trung Uy* Trang?"

"Yes. I am Trang, but I received my cleaning a couple of evenings ago."

"There is no mistake," said the voice outside. "This is

157

for you."

Trang went to the door and jerked it open. "I told you I have nothing at the dry cleaners."

The deliveryman stepped inside. "Please, believe me, sir. This is your uniform."

Trang took the garment and angrily ripped the covering from it. "This is expensive garbardine. I have nothing but khaki clothing."

Xong, in his role as the dry cleaning truck driver, was gently insistent. "Try it on. I think it is your size."

Trang instinctively felt that something unusual was taking place. He removed his shirt and slipped into the one just presented to him. "It is a trifle large in the waist."

Xong smiled. "Then you can easily have it tailored."

"Bah!" Trang exclaimed. "That costs money, and I cannot afford to wear fancy uniforms."

"Please, *Trung Uy* Trang. Check the left breast pocket."

Trang did as he was told and pulled out a wad of piasters. Frowning with confusion, he counted them. "*Cai nay la cai gi?* There is over one hundred thousand piasters here."

"That amounts to nearly a thousand dollars American," Xong said.

"But who is giving this to me? And why?" Trang asked.

"Consider it a gift from friends who sympathize with the shabby treatment you received about your promotion," Xong said. He walked to the door and opened it. "And there will be more coming."

"Who are these—these *friends*?" Trang demanded.

"Patriots who do not like to see a good Vietnamese officer slighted while the foreign dogs shower undeserved praise and rewards down on traitors!"

Trang, still confused but delighted, counted the money

158

once more. He had been right. There was a total of one hundred and ten thousand piasters. When he looked up to speak again, the dry cleaning driver was gone.

The crowd in the Ping village courtyard had become better organized. There was no pretense about the Black Eagles now being prisoners. Yet the Ping-Yan-Uen had made no moves to disarm them. Each man still had his M16 rifle.

While most of the Ping-Yan-Uen soldiers had been drawn up into a proper military formation, others had their rifles trained on Falconi and his men. Andrea, still guarded by the pair of Pings, stayed on the porch.

The *foo-koon*, as Tsang's aide-de-camp, did his duty by clapping his hands three times. All the Pings, with the exception of those watching the foreigners, bowed as Tsang stepped out of the hut onto the porch. He had changed into his ancient costume with the lacquered wooden breastplate and the antique sword. He spoke a few of the magical words used for such sacred occasions, then returned to the interior of the hut.

Andrea, from her vantage point, could easily look into the interior of the damaged building. She saw Tsang kneel before the old altar, then lean forward. She instantly recognized that he was entering a trancelike state. Andrea also realized that the fate of herself and her comrades-in-arms depended on what realizations were flashed into the Chinese mercenary's mind during that period of deep prayer and meditation.

The uncomfortable situation went on for an hour. Andrea took furtive glances into the hut. Tsang, on his knees, had bowed so low that his forehead touched the floor. Despite this awkward position, he stayed completely immobile.

The Pings, like most Orientals, had an inborn patience

159

that could sustain them through long bouts of uncertainty or physical discomfort. Even Andrea, despite her European blood, was able to endure the slow passage of time without displaying any nervousness. The same was true with Kim, the Korean marine. Another individual with stoic endurance was Ray Swift Elk, descended from Plains warriors who, themselves, could number ancestors among Asian travelers who had crossed an ancient land link between their continent and North America.

The others, however, fidgeted and began to get irritable. The worst was Archie Dobbs. "What the fuck's goin' on?" he demanded in a whisper.

"Our fate is resting on whatever Tsang learns during his prayers to the old generals," Falconi said.

Top nudged Archie. "Just act calm, for God's sake!"

"If these Pings sumbitches think they're gonna croak me without a fight, they're crazy!" Archie hissed angrily. "I don't roll over over nobody!"

"Cool it, baby," Calvin Culpepper said. "Them little dudes ain't done nothin' yet."

"Yeah?" Archie sneered. "Well, it's pretty stupid of 'em to leave us armed."

"Lord above, Archie!" Blue Richards said. "We ain't got a chance. But if they decide to bushwhack us, we'll take a shit-pot of 'em with us."

Falconi looked over at Blue. "Speaking of shit-pots, the next time I ask for a count on the enemy, I want a better answer than, 'there's a whole shit-pot full of 'em.'"

Blue was confused. "Damn, sir! That's how many of 'em they was—a whole shit-pot full."

Falconi's eyes rolled heavenward. "Between your 'shit-pots' and Kim's 'more enemy than stars in the sky,' there was no way I could make a sound tactical decision."

"But, skipper," Blue protested. "I knowed what I meant."

"Next time speak English, not Alabamese," Falconi said.

Blue grinned, "Oh, hell, you shoulda tole me to count like a damn Yankee. Then I'd tole you there was between three and four hundred o' the scrawny fuckers."

There was a sudden flurry among the Pings. Tsang stepped out of the hut and onto the porch. The guards around the Black Eagles raised their M16s until the muzzles were trained dead on Falconi and his men.

The major licked his dry lips. "This is it, guys."

Archie Dobbs scowled. "Like I said—I ain't rollin' over for no sumbitch!"

An old woman scurried up the steps and presented the captain of the Ping-Yan-Uen with a cup of hot tea. He quickly consumed the strong drink and handed back the drinking utensil. Then Tsang took several deep breaths to help him recover.

Finally he addressed his people. "I have prayed to the great Pyang Tseung! He has spoken to me in a way that was never more resolute nor comprehensible."

The *foo-koon* stepped forward. "What has he told you, Tsang *Sheung-Wai*?"

He pointed to Andrea. "That is not Chin-Sza-Tung! She is not Warrior-Sister!"

An angry gasp rose from the crowd, and the men watching the Black Eagles surged toward them.

Tsang continued. "She is Chin-Sza-Tung's little sister, and we are to call her Sai-Chin-Sza-Tung!"

The mood suddenly changed, and the Pings watching the Black Eagles became less belligerent. A couple even allowed the muzzles of their weapons to drop a little.

Then Tsang pointed over to Falconi. "Pyang Tseung has also advised me that the man who we call *Shiu-Kaau* Falconi should lead us, while Sai-Chin-Sza-Tung fights beside all of us as a *p'ang-yau-sai*—little comrade." He raised the old sword above his head. *"Gaaung-Po!"*

161

The Pings responded. "*Gaaung-Po! Gaaung-Po!*"

For a full five minutes, the area rang with the ancient battle cry of these warrior people.

Finally Tsang signaled for quiet. Then he pointed directly at Robert Falconi. "What is it that you would have us do, *Shiu-Kaau?*"

Falconi pushed his way through the guards, then walked toward the large hut as the other people politely made way for him. He stopped at the bottom of the steps and looked up at Tsang. "The first order of business is a council of war—now!"

In downtown Hanoi, the building which housed the intelligence staff of the North Vietnam army buzzed with activity. The different bureaus, ladened down with heavy paperwork assignments, functioned in the ponderous methods adopted from the administrative-happy Soviet advisors.

Maj. Truong Van, a classified message pouch under his arm, did not appear to be a happy man as he walked down the hall toward the office he shared with the KGB lieutenant colonel named Gregori Krashchenko.

He paused at the door, hesitated, then pushed it open. He tossed the canvas container over to the Russian's desk.

"What is this?" Krashchenko asked. The Soviet officer looked terrible. Red-eyed and weary in appearance, he was obviously a troubled man.

"It is a communications!" Truong snapped. "What does it look like?"

Krashchenko gave his NVA counterpart a close scrutiny, then his facial expression slowly evolved into a smile. "You seem upset about something. Could it be this message?"

Truong said nothing.

162

"Ah!" Krashchenko exclaimed. "If you are irritated, it must be because whatever is in here is good news for me, *nyet?*"

Truong remained silent.

Krashchenko slowly opened the pouch, enjoying his companion's discomfort. He leisurely pulled out the papers inside. "Did you translate this accurately?" he asked with undisguised glee.

Truong solemnly lit a cigarette.

The Russian read the words slowly, three times. Then he sat the paper down on the desktop. He pointed a finger at Truong. "You are in a lot of trouble, monkey."

Truong swallowed nervously and continued to smoke.

"There will be three things happening within a matter of days," Krashchenko said. "First will be my promotion to the rank of major general." He paused and pulled a pack of Soviet cigarettes from his uniform pocket. "The second, without a doubt, will be awarding me the Order of Suvorov for my handling of this operation." He lit his cigarette. "Do you not agree, *Tovarisch Mayor* Truong?"

Truong said nothing. He lit a fresh smoke off the dying one and continued to stare at the far wall.

Krashchenko leaned forward. "And the third happening will be your execution, you slant-eyed, noodle-slooping, pedicab-pedaling, yellow-skinned son of an Indochinese whore!"

Truong was so angry he trembled, but he knew that he dare not say anything.

Krashchenko turned his attention back to the message. "Yes, indeed! The Black Eagles and their mercenary gang are now completely surrounded and cut off. An overwhelming force of the brave Viet Cong, along with assault helicopter support, is preparing at this very moment to deliver the death blow."

Truong's hand trembled as he reached for the cigarette in his mouth. He knew that Krashchenko's revenge

163

would be complete and final—with him as much a target of the KGB killer's anger as Falconi and the Black Eagles.

Falconi, Top, Andrea, and Tsang sat on the poncho that was spread out in the tiny jungle clearing.

The Ping-Yan-Uen women and children were also nearby, hidden within a hundred and fifty meter radius of this impromptu command post. There was absolutely no question of the civilians remaining in the village. Its location was well known, and it was impossible to defend the place from air attack without the proper weaponry.

The Ping people were used to all sorts of difficulties and dangers. The word *contingency* described a big part of their culture. They always had arms, food, and other supplies in secret caches in case they had to abandon their more comfortable hamlet and head into the jungle to survive or evade a relentless, stronger enemy.

It would be a bad time for them, but they could persevere—provided they could defeat this new enemy at best, or they could break out of his tight encirclement at the least.

Falconi looked at Tsang. "You're sure you have no heavy weapons? Perhaps you've forgotten some secret location."

"I regret to say we have none," Tsang answered. "We traded them to the ARVN for uniforms." He held up his M16. "This is the best we have. But we do got plenty bullets for enemy gun."

"Do you have seven point sixty-two?" Falconi asked. "Like they use in their automatic weapons?"

"The same," Tsang assured him. "But no got nothing to shoot it with."

Andrea shook her head. "This is not good. The closest thing we have to a support weapon is Kim's M seventy-three grenade launcher."

"I'm afraid that won't do," Falconi said.

Tsang held out his hands in a helpless gesture. "We are lost without something to support our attacks and to shoot at the helicopters, oh-you-kid. What must be done?"

"That's easy to answer," Falconi said. "Somebody has to make a midnight requisition and get some heavy weaponry."

"From who?" Andrea demanded.

"The nearest supply depot belongs to the Viet Cong," Falconi answered.

Andrea smiled in mirthless humor. "Are you going to present a requisition to their quartermaster?"

"In a manner of speaking," Falconi said. He was thoughtful for a few moments. "Archie, Ray Swift Elk, and I are going to make a clandestine social call on the VC and take what we need."

Andrea opened her eyes wide. "You mean you're going to sneak into their camp and steal a couple of machine guns?"

"And maybe a mortar or two as well," Falconi said matter-of-factly.

"Base plates are very heavy," Andrea reminded him.

Falconi shrugged. "I didn't say we'd get *big* mortars."

Tsang rolled his eyes in consternation. "It cannot be done, oh-you-kid! It is too much danger!"

"It's not only difficult, it's impossible!" Andrea insisted.

Falconi stood up. "The difficult takes us awhile, the impossible a bit longer." He winked at Andrea. "Pardon me. I have to go round up Archie and Ray."

"You'll need more than just the three of you," Andrea said.

Falconi shook his head. "We'd never make it through

165

VC country with more people. Three's the right number. We'll just have to carry what we can. See you later."

Tsang watched the American major walk away. He called out to him. *"Chuk nei hang-wan!"*

Andrea gripped her M16 rifle tighter. "There's not enough luck in the world for what he's going to try to do."

CHAPTER TWELVE

Major Falconi squatted behind the huge jungle fern, his M16 rifle gripped tightly in his strong hands. He glanced to the rear and caught sight of Ray Swift Elk a scant five meters away. Turning back, he strained his eyes trying to see Archie Dobbs.

The Falcon was stripped for action. Wearing his soft cap and carrying nothing but the barest of essentials— ammo, canteen and a knife—he was ready for the do-or-die mission he was on.

It was late afternoon, with the sun beginning its rapid plunge toward the horizon as is typical in the tropics. That was the one thing that the Falcon disliked most about that part of the world—those short evenings. He could remember when he'd been a young boy and his father had been stationed at Fort Snelling, Minnesota. The winters had been absolutely hell, but those long, wonderful Midwest summer evenings lasted past ten o'clock at night.

Archie Dobbs's face, streaked with green and black camouflage paint like Falconi's and Swift Elk's, suddenly appeared in the vegetation. He signalled for Falconi to follow him. The major turned and repeated the gesture for the Sioux intelligence sergeant behind him.

The trio, which had stopped when Archie perceived some disturbance ahead, resumed their slow trek. They had left the newly established base camp at dawn, some thirteen hours earlier. Moving through the jungle toward the Viet Cong hamlet at an incredibly slow pace, the small team had traveled only ten kilometers in all that time.

Falconi's plan was to arrive at a good observation point before dark and settle in to observe the target area. He wanted to remain at least twenty-four hours in this perilous position to observe whatever routine the Red guerrillas followed in their everyday living.

The Black Eagle commander also wanted to pick out the routes he and his two companions would follow when they entered the place to steal whatever heavy weaponry would be avalable to them. Despite having attacked the camp, they didn't know the exact locations of arms caches or weapons storage areas. It is rather difficult to take note of local layouts, when the unfriendlies are doing their best to blow you away.

The most important thing at this point, however, was to avoid any contact with VC patrols or personnel. Even if such an encounter resulted in the enemy's being eliminated, it would still be a disaster. The old saying that dead men tell no tales is as wrong as wrong can be. A slain guard or ambushed patrol gives out plenty of information. It's an obvious giveaway that someone a bit menacing is in the area and can result in dire consequences—especially when there are only three interlopers facing an entire Viet Cong battalion.

Falconi, walking slowly and exercising extreme care, kept his eyes both on the ground and on Archie as they eased through the dense brush. Suddenly Archie signaled and ducked. Falconi quickly repeated the gesture for Swift Elk's benefit, then dropped silently to the ground.

Within seconds came the sounds of walking men.

Falconi guessed there must be at least a half dozen Viet Cong. The enemy spoke to each other in low-pitched voices, showing they were being careful, yet did not expect any of their enemies to be near.

The rustling of vegetation grew louder until it was evident the strangers were approaching the three Black Eagles' hidden positions. Falconi pressed himself closer to the ground in an instinctive effort to become less visible.

Suddenly the VC were beside him. But from the tone of their conversation, he could tell they couldn't see him through the heavy bushes.

Then they stopped.

"Cai nay la cai gi?"

"Toi muon cau tieu."

Falconi knew one of them had to take a piss.

"Duroc."

"Cam on ong, Thurong-si."

The man standing nearest Falconi turned. There was a sound of rustling cloth, then suddenly a stream of urine snaked through the heavy leaves and splattered down close to the American officer's head. Muddy piss splashed up into his face, but Falconi dared not move.

He closed his eyes and took it.

The VC finally emptied his bladder and, after rearranging his trousers, turned back to his buddies. *"Toi Tiec."*

"Di thi di!"

The patrol moved away until the area was silent again. Falconi looked toward Archie and saw the scout grinning at him. The major shoved his fist forward and raised the middle finger in salute.

Archie grinned wider, winked, then signaled to move out once again. Falconi, with Swift Elk behind him, followed.

169

The major was glad the VC hadn't had to take a crap.

"Dry cleaning."

Lieutenant Trang looked toward the door. "*Moi ong vao ngoi choi.*"

Xong entered the room. "*Cam on ong.*" He lay the clothes bag on the bed and took a seat. "How are you, lieutenant?"

"Curious," Trang answered.

Xong smiled. "No doubt."

Trang took a long, meaningful look at the large sack. "I am not a fool," he said. "And that means there's a couple of things that have to be brought out into the open. *Ong hieu toi duoc khong?*"

"I understand," Xong answered.

"The first is that I am disgusted with a system which does not reward hard work and long, loyal service," Trang said. "I do not consider myself a traitor. But even the most faithful dog will take only so many kicks."

"Of course," Xong commented.

"And the second is that I realize you represent either the Communists or some other group which wants to topple the South Vietnamese government, *khong?*"

Xong smiled. "Does it make any difference to you who sends me?"

Trang was silent for several moments. Then he looked straight into Xong's eyes. "No."

"*Murn ong*, you are an intelligent man," Xong said. "If you cannot gain rank, you at least shall have plenty of money."

"What do you require of me?" Trang asked.

"You are assigned to duty at MAC V Headquarters, *khong?*"

"Yes. I am in charge of the interior guard there."

Xong leaned forward. "Does that mean you are able to

170

move about quite freely within the building?"

"Of course. That is part of my responsibilities."

"You hear many things then."

Trang nodded. "I sometimes take a position in the rooms where meetings are being held in order to insure that proper security precautions are being observed. Thus, I know many things that have happened through hearing conversations and oral reports. There are times, as well, where I would be able to study classified documents." He went to the table beside the bed and mixed a couple of drinks. "I also am able to learn of certain activities that are occurring at any particular moment. And that includes future operations and missions."

Xong took the glass. "If my superiors are kept fully informed, you will find many hundreds of thousands of piasters within your grasp."

"Informed of what?"

"Anything you could give us," Xong answered.

"There is much. I would waste a lot of time trying to keep track of everything," Trang said. "The result would be to flood you with great deals of unnecessary information."

Xong took a sip of the drink. "Tell me, Lieutenant Trang, what do you know of the special detachment which is call the Black Eagles?"

Trang didn't hesitate. "They are on a mission in the north in Operational Area Bravo near where the borders of Laos, North Vietnam, and South Vietnam converge."

"And they are in difficulties at the moment," Xong added.

"Yes. There has been no communications with them for several days," Trang said. "How did you know that?"

"Never mind. I want you to concentrate on Major Falconi and his men until further orders."

"Ong o dong?"

171

Xong stood up. "There is fifty thousand piasters in the pocket of that tunic," he said pointing to the package on the bed. "And that is only the start." He sat his glass down and went directly to the door. *"Chao ong."*

Trang raised his glass. *"Chao ong."* He watched Xong leave, then went to the package and ripped it open. A well-made officer's tunic, complete with rank and other insignia, was inside. Trang reached into the left breast pocket and pulled out the money. He smiled to himself. *"Murn ong!"*

Falconi, peering through the binoculars, studied the Viet Cong camp in the waning light. After less than an hour of observation, he had come to several conclusions.

The most disturbing one was that a massive offensive operation was in the offing. That was easy to figure out from the frantic activities. There were several lines of troops drawing supplies, while others cleaned weapons and prepared more combat hardware. There were also constant inspections by squad and platoon leaders.

The Viet Cong unit, obviously of multi-company size, was also going to employ helicopters in their effort. There had been a work detail preparing two landing pads at the near end of the camp. They would have probably liked to have more, but time and space limited them to the pair. At least there was some advantage to the Black Eagles in that. It would take longer to pick up and return troops from missions. A Russian MI-4 chopper carried approximately one squad. That meant if a platoon were to be sent out, only half could be picked up at one time, utilizing two of the aircraft. The first pair would have to pick up their burdens, then hover while the last duo loaded up.

As Falconi continued to study the Viet Cong opponents, he also came to another realization. This was one hell of a good unit. Disciplined, trained hard and experienced, the men responded quickly and efficiently to lower-unit leaders who gave the impression of being veteran combat commanders.

These are tough mothers, his thoughts told him, *and, like Archie Dobbs, they're not going to roll over for anybody!*

Falconi lowered the binoculars and crawled back to Archie and Swift Elk. When he reached them, he whispered urgently, "I'm changing things."

"What's up, skipper?" Archie asked.

"We can't give those guys any extra time," Falconi said. "We'll have to get in there, steal what we can, and get back to the others as quickly as possible."

"No twenty-four hours of spyin' on 'em, huh, skipper?" Archie asked.

"I'm afraid that time is one luxury we don't have much of anymore," Falconi remarked. "We'll have to learn as much as we can of their routine between now and complete darkness."

Swift Elk, with the professional curiosity of a trained intelligence noncommissioned officer, asked, "How come the rush?"

"What we have here is an elite hunter-killer battalion," Falconi explained. "And they're getting ready to jump straight down our throats. If we sit here for twenty-four hours, we may find ourselves sneaking into an empty camp, with those bastards out kicking hell out of the rest of the detachment and the Pings, too."

"Then we go in tonight?" Archie asked.

"Yeah," Falconi answered.

"Did you spot their arms dump?" Swift Elk asked.

Falconi shook his head. "I'm afraid not. We'll have to hunt for it in the dark."

"Jeez!" Archie exclaimed.

Falconi winked at Swift Elk. "Well, as Custer said when he saw all those Indians, 'Don't take any prisoners, men.'"

The Sioux smiled grimly. "Custer's shit was weak, skipper."

Falconi grinned back. "So's ours."

Captain Sprosty stood in the operations hut located at the end of the small airfield that sat just inside the border of North Vietnam.

Nine other Czechoslovakian pilots were with him. These men, all lieutenants and warrant officers, wore Soviet khaki uniforms with Czech epaulets mounted on the shoulders.

Sprosty was ecstatic as he began his talk. "*Dobry den, piloti*, are you ready for the mission?"

"*Ano, kapitan!*" they answered correctly and loudly in unison. Even in the training of their pilots, the Communist system did not encourage individuality. The Communist hierarchy discovered that aviation personnel who thought for themselves generally ended up flying their planes or helicopters across international borders and landing in the West. Thus, these Czech pilots responded as one unit in the manner in which they had been schooled and trained by the East European military establishment.

"Excellent, comrades," Sprosty said. "Lieutenant Somad and I have already completed one combat sortie against the American gangsters and their Chinese bandit friends. The two of us flew through the hell of their anti-aircraft fire and destroyed much of their base camp."

Somad, who could remember nothing of AA defenses but plenty about the obvious noncombatant women and children they had shot up, wisely said nothing. Young officers in the Czech military did not receive promotions or the coveted Order of the Red Banner Medal for speaking up too truthfully under such circumstances.

"Now let us review our mission for tomorrow," Sprosty said. "My ship and Somad's will act as fire support. Mine with the guad-Goryunov machine guns and Somad with the rocket launcher will be in radio contact with the Viet Cong ground control. The rest of you will each carry a squad to the designated landing areas at the rice paddies near the Chinese village. There will be eight of you making two trips, thus our noble comrades are going to be able to put an entire company into action. You will hover above the paddies at about one or two meters and allow the men to jump from the helicopters onto the soft mud below. Then you will fly to the orbit point north of the village and wait until you are called in to retrieve the Viet Cong."

"And their prisoners, *kapitan!*" Somad added quickly.

Sprosty chuckled. "Well put, *Podporucik* Somad! And do not forget the cadavers of the Americans that intelligence wants us to bring out, too!"

The other pilots joined in the laughter.

The Czech commander continued. "You are hand-picked for this difficult job. And I'm sure that you, like myself, are looking forward to tomorrow's action. After years of stagnant maneuvers and training exercises in Czechoslovakia and our Warsaw Pact neighbors' homelands, we are ready for combat. This is the real thing without play enemies. And we will at last have the opportunity to kill the opponents of world socialism. Do your duty! *Potlacit americki*—Crush the Americans!"

A full, bright moon lit the area at intervals when the clouds went away for awhile. If the sky had been clear all the time, Falconi's mission would have turned into one big bust. As it was, he and his two companions were forced back into the shadows occasionally.

It was now oh two hundred hours. The darkness permitted them to leave their initial hiding place and take up a position at the jungle edge. They had spent the time checking on the sentry routine used by the Viet Cong. After watching several reliefs come and go, it became obvious the guards were changed every two hours.

The plan now was to wait for the present sentries to be relieved, then let fifteen minutes go by before infiltrating the enemy encampment. It would mean taking out one sentry and hoping like hell the corpse wasn't discovered until the next relief came on duty. If things went well, they would have an hour and forty-five minutes to search out the weapons storage area, take what they needed, and haul ass back to the others.

Footsteps and soft murmuring alerted the trio of Black Eagles. They observed as a new guard took the old one's place. Falconi checked his luminous watch dial, then settled back to wait.

After a quarter of an hour, he whispered to Archie and Swift Elk. "Let's go!"

They silently got to their feet and glided across the expanse of open area between the jungle and the village. The Viet Cong guard listlessly walked his post, his head downcast as he absentmindedly performed what he considered a useless job in a safe area.

Falconi reached into his large side pocket and pulled out the garrots. In a swift, sure movement, the wire device went over the Red's head and bit deep into his neck. The VC suffocated quickly in his own blood. The Falcon motioned the others forward with a nod of his head.

They walked quietly among the huts, stopping often to listen. Mostly they heard the deep breathing of sleeping men, or low-toned conversation of more restless ones.

Falconi had made a wild guess during the last moments

176

of daylight. There had been a certain hut that seemed to be a workshop of some sorts. The Black Eagle guessed that since the Viet Cong had no vehicles or other machinery, the place must be used to repair or perform maintenance on weapons. If that were the case, it would also be where surplus or crew-served weapons were stored.

Unfortunately, the target was located beside the one building where there would be night-long activity—the guardhouse. Although the sentries off duty would probably be sleeping, there would always be a noncommissioned officer who stayed awake, as well as the inevitable restless souls who would rather sit up and talk than try to get any shut-eye.

Falconi, in the lead, reached the edge of the shanty nearest the guardhouse. He dropped to the ground and eased his head around the edge of the crude building for a quick look-see. Then he ducked back.

"Shit!" he whispered.

"What's up, skipper?" Swift Elk asked.

"The hut where the guards are staying is wide open on three sides. We'll have to sneak the long way around and come in the back way."

Archie Dobbs wasn't worried. "Let's do it."

Falconi motioned for them to follow him. They retraced their steps a few meters before turning off into the billeting area. Now the Black Eagles were in the dead center of the VC barracks. That meant that chances of running into some nocturnal wanderer increased even more.

Falconi, staying in the lead, proceeded as fast as he could. There was now less than an hour and a half before the next guard relief would come on. That would mean an immediate discovery of the dead sentry.

When they reached the buildings that had no sides, the trio of Black Eagles were finally forced to slow down.

They had to crawl on their bellies, inch by inch, past the billets. At the final barracks, there was some eager beaver sitting up reading by candlelight. He was so close to the edge of the hut that Falconi could make out the Vietnamese wording on the document that had attracted the Viet Cong's attention. It was a treatise by Ho Chi Minh about Communist triumphs being inevitable in Southeast Asia.

At that particular time, Messrs. Falconi, Dobbs, and Swift Elk were doing their best to spoil these particular predictions.

A tense twenty minutes passed before they finally reached an area where they could once again get to their feet. They couldn't afford to even spare a couple of minutes to catch their breaths as they once again began to work their way back to the arms shack.

The Viet Cong NCO bumped into Falconi as he stepped around the corner of the building.

Falconi recognized the man as the one who had been posting the guards. He was probably heading out for a surprise inspection of the posts. That was something the Black Eagle commander hadn't taken into consideration.

The VC's eyes popped open as his sleepy mind tried to comprehend what he saw. A tall American stood there in plain sight. It was as stunningly surprising to the Red as if a two-headed dragon had suddenly appeared.

Falconi, on the other hand, was expecting the worst—and he reacted accordingly. His right hand, formed for a straight knuckle jab, flew forward instinctively toward the solar plexis in a "panther" punch. The sturdy fist hit just below the Viet Cong's ribs, causing the Commie to give out with a brief whoosh of air before collapsing.

Falconi grabbed the man in both arms like he'd fallen madly in love with him, then lowered his victim to the ground. The major quickly drew his razor-sharp stiletto and sliced it across the jugular veins in efficient movements.

178

Now they would really have to haul ass. There were no less than two of the dead sons of bitches around just waiting for somebody to stumble across them.

When they reached the arms shack, they found that the proverbial Lady Luck was not only smiling down on them, she was laughing to beat the band. The back wall that Falconi had spotted on his initial reconnaissance proved to be part of a well-stocked arms room. The weapons he had seen in the machine shop area were but a small part of the overall supply.

The three eased into the pitch dark of the crude chamber. Falconi produced a flashlight and turned it on. Giving silent orders by pointing, he directed Archie and Swift Elk to each grab one of the light machine guns that were sitting there. The weapons looked as if they had been waiting for the Black Eagles to come fetch them. These were Chinese 7.62 millimeter type 53 which were copies of the Soviet DPMs. Falconi's eager eyes swept the room for other goodies, then stopped on a sight that made his heart leap to his mouth.

There, in all its glory, leaning against the far wall was a Hotchkiss-Brandt 60 millimeter trench mortar. This simple French weapon, designed to be used by one man, would be a perfect replacement for Kim's grenade launcher. Not only was it more powerful, it was even simpler to operate. Falconi picked it up and slung it over his shoulder. There were also some bandoleers of the small shells used in the tubular firing device. Loading himself down, he motioned his two companions to leave. Because of the Pings having plenty of 7.62 ammo cached in the jungle surrounding their village, there was no need of toting any of that off.

Once outside, they paused only long enough to rearrange the thatched wall used for their entry to conceal the theft as long as possible. Then the Black Eagles turned their attention to getting the hell out of the camp and begin the slow trek back to their comrades.

Falconi took them on a more direct route back toward the jungle. It would have been impossible to trace their steps back along the original route. Besides, the most basic rule of combat in Vietnam was to never, never follow the same trail twice.

They reached the edge of the billeting area and paused to get a bearing on any guards. After a scant five minutes, the sentry appeared, walking in a slow pace along the outer perimeter of the camp.

Swift Elk, the scion of prairie warrior stealth, moved silently but swiftly into action. He was like a living shadow as he closed the distance between himself and his quarry. A brawny arm locked around the VC's neck, cutting off the blood supply to the brain. Even as the guerrilla lost consciousness, the Sioux's knife ended the struggle.

Swift Elk quickly returned to the stolen machine gun and was joined by Falconi and Archie as they trod carefully out of the Viet Cong base.

By the time they hit the edge of the jungle and continued on into the concealment offered by the foliage, the first red rays of the rising sun were easing up over the horizon.

CHAPTER THIRTEEN

Master Sergeant Gordon was as worried as a second lieutenant called to a company commander's meeting.

He had been left in charge of a unit cut off from any communications with friendly forces while surrounded deep in enemy territory. And, if that wasn't bad enough, the force he now commanded was about as unconventional as it could possibly be.

Most of his unit was made up of a strange people called Ping-Yan-Uen whose customs and history comprised generations of mercenary soldiering. In the past, they had not only shown a tendency to fight for either the richest side—or one that had a sure-fire chance to win— but they demonstrated a complete disregard for their own lives through a belief that, should they be killed, they would be elevated to an afterworld in which they would:

(a) advise their living descendents on martial matters; (b) be able to have a hell of a good time fighting in battles in which not only the wounded, but the *dead* recovered afterward; and (c) they would have numerous beautiful women to look after their physical needs, along with plenty of the best food, quarters, and recreation that a paradise could offer.

It is very difficult to keep people like that alive.

But, at that particular point, Top had to give more consideration to the tactical situation than the religious one. So he turned to his nearly twenty years of military experience and put on his thinking cap.

The veteran sergeant knew the best way to deal with the problems would be to melt into the jungle and break down into small units for an escape-and-evasion maneuver that would carry most, if not all, of them back to safer areas.

But, unfortunately that was impossible.

The Pings' women and children were also caught up in this latest problem. No matter how suicidal the men might become during battle, the idea of having their families slaughtered was not as appealing as their own deaths. Thus, Top was hampered by this large contingent of noncombatants which made escape into the wilds impossible. He had to do the next best thing. Prepare for a serious offensive from a strong enemy and hope to hang on long enough for something like a complete miracle to happen.

This was becoming Standing Operating Procedure for the Black Eagles as of late.

The only way for the enemy to effectively reach them was across the open area of the abandoned rice paddies the Black Eagles had used for a drop zone during their initial entry into the operation. With this distinct area to defend, the master sergeant had organized his force and ordered them to dig in among the heavy tropical vegetation that stood between the open area and the village that had been shot up by the Red choppers. After that, there was nothing to do but wait for developments.

Top sat up his command post in the center of the defenses. He shared this crude headquarters, actually not much more than an enlarged foxhole, with the Ping captain, Tsang, and Andrea Thuy.

Tsang, although patient, was curious. "When *Shiu-*

Kaau Falconi come back?"

Top shook his head. "Hard to tell. It'll be rough going both ways."

"Especially if the VC are patrolling heavily," Andrea said.

"I don't care of VC patrol," Tsang said. "I worry for the helicopters to come back. We got to get machine guns *i-ka faal ti*!"

"You're right," Top replied. He patted his M16. "These might help a little—damned little—but we need something that'll punch into those flying machines."

"We got bullets, need machine guns," Tsang repeated in the Ping custom of using repetition to get certain points across.

"Falconi'll bring the weapons," Top assured him. He tried to sound as optimistic as possible despite knowing that, between the Viet Cong on the ground and the helicopters in the sky, there were some very hairy moments ahead of them.

Tsang looked at Andrea. "How do you feel about things, Sai-Chin-Sza-Tung?"

"I have great confidence in *Shiu-Kaau* Falconi," Andrea answered sincerely. "He has volunteered to go on a very dangerous mission to bring about a victory."

Tsang sighed. "Everything bad now. Men don't want to die if women are caught by Viet Cong sumbitches. They fight hard. Don't worry."

Top felt a little better at hearing that. At least the Pings could be counted on to pay a bit more attention to the tactical side of the battle, rather than the death-or-glory bit they found so attractive.

But they were all still up to their eyeballs in trouble, nevertheless.

Sprosty turned back on the throttle while pushing

183

down gently on the collective to lower his helicopter down to the landing pad at the edge of the village.

The landing signalman, a Czech sergeant who had been attached to the VC as instructor, hurried under the still spinning main rotors and leaped into the fuselage. He scrambled up into the pilot's compartment. "*Tezkost, kapitan,*" he said.

"What's the problem?" Sprosty asked.

"The Viet Cong comrades found three of their guards dead this morning," the man said. "It appears the area was infiltrated by the enemy last night."

"*Kolik?*"

"They don't know how many, *kapitan*. Nor what they accomplished except to sneak into the area. Do you suppose it might mean an attempt to attack our aircraft here on the ground? Perhaps they didn't know we have an aerodrome to use in the north."

"How many men did you say were killed?" Sprosty asked.

"They found three this morning. Two privates and a sergeant. All had been detailed to the garrison guard."

"Only three?" Sprosty asked. "Doesn't sound like a big problem to me."

"But, *kapitan*, it appears as if some mischief was attempted," the other Czech protested. "Though our comrades made a quick check around the camp and found no disturbance."

"Bah!" Sprosty said. "It was probably nothing more than a fight between some soldiers. Somebody made a play for another's woman. Or perhaps gambling comes into it. Orientals are notorious at games of chance." He looked around at the camp. "Why would anyone risk their lives to sneak into an armed camp to randomly kill only three people? But, evidently the incident didn't alter any plans. It appears as if today's operation is going

184

off as scheduled."

"*Ano, kapitan,*" the sergeant replied in the affirmative.

"Then let's not waste time. I will call on the Viet Cong commander while you see to getting the troops on the helicopters."

"*Ano, kapitan!*"

Sprosty unbuckled himself and swung out of the cockpit. He took a couple of strides across the troop compartment and dropped to the ground. He spotted the VC commander just off the landing pad. The Czech approached and saluted. "We are ready for action, comrade major."

"And so are we," Major Dnang replied.

"My sergeant tells me there was a disturbance in the camp last night," Sprosty said.

"Yes," Dnang admitted. "Three of our guard detail were killed. We haven't had time to determine the reason for the occurrence."

Sprosty shrugged. "It doesn't seem serious, comrade major."

Dnang, a veteran of almost fifteen years of fighting, spoke coldly. "I consider it very serious any time interlopers enter my command and kill some of our men."

"I did not mean to belittle the situation, comrade," Sprosty said in a soothing tone. "It could very possibly have been the result of an argument between some of your soldiers."

Dnang ignored him. "The helicopters are loaded, and I see the other two are waiting to come in and pick up more men. I think we'd better get a move on."

"Of course, comrade," Sprosty said. "We Czechs are anxious to get into action this morning."

"Then let's have no more discussion," Dnang said

185

walking toward the aircraft.

"Take ten," Falcon said breathlessly.

Although there was no time to waste, he, Archie, and Swift Elk had reached a point in their fatigue that a brief rest was absolutely essential. The three went into a tiny clearing and settled down on the soft, muddy earth for a breather.

"How far have we gone?" Falconi asked Archie.

"About five klicks, I figure," Archie replied. "At least that's what I estimate. I hope I'm right."

"If you say five klicks, then it's five klicks," Falconi said out of respect for Archie's tracking and orientation skills. "Damn! These things are a load, aren't they?"

"Sure are, skipper," Swift Elk said. "Particularly when we gotta carry 'em while tryin' to move fast and not make noise."

"I'd like to push ahead with more speed, but there's too big a chance of VC patrols in the area," Falconi said.

Archie gave his commander's burden a curious look. "I ain't had a chance to ask you, skipper, but what the hell is that thing you scarfed up anyhow?"

"It's a small French commando mortar," Falconi answered. "This thing was probably taken by the Viet Minh a decade or so ago. I fired one in the weapons familiarization training phase during the officers' Special Forces course at Bragg."

"Looks like a thick stove pipe," Swift Elk said unimpressed.

"That's about all this particular model is," Falconi admitted. "There's another type with a small base plate. To fire that one you just drop a round down the tube."

"What about that one?" Archie asked.

"You load it the same way, but it won't fire until you pull the lanyard," Falconi explained.

"Damn, skipper!" Swift Elk exclaimed in professional curiosity. "What about aiming stakes and all that? How the hell do you lay the damn thing in?"

"You see this white line on the tube? Well, just use that to aim toward your target. You simply set the thing on the ground between your legs and guess the right angle to hold it—then let 'er rip!"

Archie chuckled. "Not real scientific, skipper."

"Maybe not," Falconi said. "But once you get used to this baby, she'll drop 'em close enough to get the bad guys. Don't worry about that."

Swift Elk chuckled. "Ol' Kim's gonna be real jealous if that takes the place of his M79 grenade launcher."

Falconi winked at the Indian NCO. "I'll just tell him I got this thing to augment him."

"You're a real diplomat, skipper," Archie said grinning.

Falconi got to his feet. "Let's go, guys. We got to get back to the Ping village before the VC do."

The three resumed their difficult trek through the clinging vines and other thick brush that seemed to have a mind of its own as it pushed back against their efforts.

"Hold it!" Swift Elk said.

"What the hell's the matter?" Archie asked.

Swift Elk was quiet for a couple of seconds. "Hear 'em? Helicopters!"

"Yeah," Archie said. "And look. Just like them two the other day. They're headin' straight for the Ping village."

Swift Elk looked up at the choppers through the canopy of trees. "And we can't do a damn thing about it."

Archie glared at his useless machine gun. "Jeez: If we only had ammo for these babies."

"It's back there in the Pings' caches," Falconi said. "We won't be able to help much until we mate this stuff up."

187

"I just hope there's somebody back there to help when we do get back," Archie said.

"Screw noise discipline!" Falconi said. "Let's haul ass!"

The two Czechoslovak choppers eased down behind the rice paddies on the far side from the village. The troops inside immediately disembarked and took up positions facing the Ping-Yan-Uen hamlet.

Once they were given the wave-off by the specially trained landing signalmen, Sprosty and the other pilot climbed back into the sky to make another run for more VC.

The Viet Cong commander watched the first choppers go and smiled to himself as the next two came in. He waited until they, too, had unloaded and gone back for another group of men.

His superbly trained troops were now in position. He blew on his whistle. "Platoon leaders, move out!"

The first line of attack advanced slowly toward the distant village.

Sparks Martin studied the terrain through the binoculars. He continued to observe while he spoke. "Looks like a coupla platoons, Top."

"Right," Top said using his own lenses. "And no doubt those goddamned choppers are going back for more."

"We can handle what's comin' now," Sparks said.

"Sure," Top said. "And they know it too. That's why they're taking their time coming across those paddies."

"And using all the available cover while they're at it," Sparks added.

A shot exploded from the perimeter, then a half dozen more.

"Cease fire! Cease fire!" Top yelled. "They're not in range yet."

Calvin Culpepper's voice came over the radio. "No sweat, Top. A coupla Pings got excited over here. We calmed 'em down. Out."

Top had put Calvin in charge of Fire Team Alpha when he'd assumed over all command during Falconi's absence. He knew he'd made a good choice. The black veteran sergeant didn't let any situation get out of hand when he was in the driver's seat.

There was a couple of distant pops from the Viet Cong. Top laughed. "Sounds like they're anxious, too."

"Can't say as I blame 'em," Sparks said. "If I was goin' into combat against a bunch o' jokers I'd soon outnumber two or three to one, I'd be anxious to get on with it, too."

Sprosty's chopper went in and barely hit the ground when the next squad of VC rushed into the interior. The Czech sergeant waved him off, and the pilot climbed skyward. He spoke into his radio. *"Pripraven?"*

"Ano!" came back young Lieutenant Somad's voice.

"Let's go!" Sprosty said. The two choppers swung on course and headed back for the rice paddies. "And don't forget! After we drop this load off, we go to the attack!"

Somad's voice trembled with excitement. *"Pripraven!"*

"Oh, God!" Archie said. "There goes more of 'em."

"They're the same ones," Falconi said. "I noticed the numbers on the fuselages before."

"Must be flying their assault forces in shifts, huh, skipper?" Swift Elk asked.

"I'd say so," Falconi said. "C'mon, let's step it up."

The three, soaked in sweat with every muscle aching in

protest, increased the pace in the wild hope of getting the extra weapons to their friends in time to be of help.

Top watched the next helicopter lift come in and disgorge its human load. He cursed under his breath. "I wish we had something we could reach those bastards with."

"At least we had time to dig in good," Sparks said.

Top picked up his radio. "Bravo, this is Top. Over."

"This is Bravo. Over," answered Kim.

"How are the Ping civilians doing? Over."

"They went way back into hiding area," Kim answered. "Helicopters no reach them unless they make lucky shots into jungle. How things look up there? Over."

Top looked up in time to see the two helicopter gunships turn in toward his position. "The shit's about to hit the fan. Out."

Sprosty threw the MI-4 into a steep turn, then swung toward the target area. He flew with a slightly downtilted attitude, giving the four machine guns under the fuselage a clear field of fire at the ground. When he was within three hundred meters of the Ping village, he pressed the trigger switch. The rapid chugging of the weapons made the chopper shudder a bit, and he had to compensate for the disturbance with extra play on the rudders.

He continued firing until he could see the tracers crashing into the jungle on the far side of the village. He pulled back, banked and headed out of range of any potential anti-aircraft fire. He spotted young Lieutenant Somad, wisps of smoking whipping out of the rocket-firing tubes, sending the small missiles streaking down

190

into the same area.

Then he excitedly twisted the throttle to maximum as he rushed to get into position for his next run.

Thick oily smoke blew over Top Gordon. He spat and rubbed his eyes, then got back on his radio. "Alpha, report. Over."

"They come in close, but not close enough. We're okay so far. Over," Calvin said.

"Bravo, report. Over."

"We take direct hit on Ping position," Kim said. "Six casualty. Ever'body else okay. Over."

"Roger. Out," Top said.

"Here they come again!" Sparks yelled.

M16s barked loudly as the defenders made superhuman efforts to hit some vulnerable part on the approaching helicopters. But it was useless.

"Get down!" Top yelled.

The whole world seemed to evolve into a rapid series of explosions as the machine gun bullets pounded the ground in a steady stream. Geysers of earth erupted, and ricochets sang out as the myriad of slugs that didn't strike something solid zinged out into nothingness.

There was a short moment of silence before the next ship roared in.

A series of loud detonations rocked the atmosphere for a short but brutal five seconds.

Then, again, silence.

Top came up out of his fighting hole quickly, looking for any target of opportunity. But there were none. He glanced over toward Sparks Martin's position. "How do things look, Sparks?"

There was no answer.

Top leaped up and rushed over to the radio operator.

There was nothing left but a smoking, blackened gash in the earth. Top glanced at a nearby brush. A scorched M16 rifle butt protruded from under it. He walked to it and reached down, pulling the weapon out.

A human hand still clutched the upper hand guard.

Top noted the eagle and another tattoo—that was the only bit of flesh left of PO, 2c Sparks Martin.

Malpractice McCorckel appeared at Top's side. The medic picked up the hand. He walked a few meters away, then scooped a deep hole in the soft jungle earth with his boot. After dropping the only mortal remains of the Navy man into the earthen cavity, he covered it up.

Top watched him dully. "Not exactly full military honors."

"Not exactly a complete corpse either," Malpractice said. "But that's the best—" He looked skyward. "Oh, shit! Here they come again!"

Both Black Eagles dove for cover as the new aerial attack roared in on them.

Archie led the way with Falconi and Swift Elk behind him. "What the hell are they hittin' the village with?" he asked.

"Machine guns and rockets," Falconi answered. He ran with a great deal of difficulty, the commando mortar's twenty-two pounds pulling him over to one side. He had shifted the bandoleer of small shells to the opposite shoulder to compensate for the uneven load, but the going was still rough.

Swift Elk, moving in a close third position behind his commander, spoke in a low, angry voice. "They're softenin' the guys up for the ground troops. Then it'll be small arms and bayonets."

"Christ!" Archie said. "Our boys won't stand a

chance. It'll be worse than what happened at the VC hamlet."

"We gotta hurry!" Falconi urged them.

"What if we run into flanking patrols, skipper?" Archie asked. He indicated his machine gun. "This won't be much help."

"Then throw it at the sons of bitches," Falconi said. "Let's go!"

CHAPTER FOURTEEN

The loud reports of M16 rifles along the Black Eagles and Pings' defense line broke out sporadically, then gradually built up as the first ranks of Viet Cong infantry came within range.

The initial enemy lines caught pure hell as the 5.56 millimeter slugs ripped through their combat formations. The small men buckled under the fusillade's impact, falling in piles before their friends farther back caught up with them and took some of the pressure off by adding to their own volume of return firing.

Andrea Thuy, aka Sai-Chin-Sza-Tung, kept her M16 rifle on semi-automatic fire. She carefully selected her targets, taking quick but accurate sight pictures before squeezing the trigger. Each shot from the beautiful Eurasian woman dumped an unfortunate Red into the mud of the rice paddies.

Malpractice, next to her in his own fighting position, was performing his special brand of defensive firing. This was done by spraying out short firebursts on full automatic as he swept up and down the enemy ranks in a regular rhythm. He noted Andrea's successes and gave out an admiring whistle. "Way to go!" he hollered over to her as he saw one enemy guerrilla throw up his hands and collapse under the slamming of a slug from her rifle.

Andrea, who took killing Communists very seriously, did not want to be distracted from her task, so she refrained from acknowledging his praise. She spotted an individual who was obviously a squad or platoon leader. He gave various arm and hand signals to keep a small unit moving toward the Black Eagles and Pings. Andrea aimed long and carefully at the potato-masher type Soviet grenade he had hanging from his equipment harness. She took up the slack on the trigger and waited for him to turn a bit more to the front so that she had better than a three-quarter view of his torso. When he did, she closed down on the trigger.

The round hit the grenade, exploding it in a sheet of orange flame. The top half of the VC disappeared, and three men near him were swept from their feet by the ensuing shower of shrapnel. One, only wounded, struggled to his knees in shock and confusion. He staggered around a bit, clutching at the bloody wounds that seeped through his pajamalike uniform.

One more round from Andrea's M16 punched through his forehead, throwing him over onto his back in an awkward, undignified position.

Back farther, Chun Kim, wielding his M79 grenade launcher, had a perplexing problem. If he fired with the weapon at too high an angle, the small projectiles would reach the zenith of their trajectories, then plummet straight down to bury themselves deep in the rice paddy mud. When they struck the ground, the rounds ended up so deep in the wet earth that their explosive force was nearly halved.

After seeing several of the enemy quickly recover from detonations that were more wet earth than metal, the Korean marine came up with a novel—and dangerous—idea.

He crawled out of his foxhole and slithered on his belly

to the trunk of a nearby tree. Then, keeping himself on the far side from the enemy, he stood up. At his height of five feet, six inches tall, it seemed he would be able to fire at a flatter angle into the groups of Viet Cong.

He quickly leaned around the tree, sighted, and fired. The grenade streaked out and smacked down flatly. When it exploded, it sent a Charlie into a low somersault, one detached leg spinning crazily through the air.

The determined Korean managed to get off half a dozen more telling shots, until he was spotted. The next time he attempted to send a projectile flying toward the enemy, a half dozen bullets exploded into the tree he was using for cover. Bark and splinters sprayed out from the incoming rounds, stinging his face. Kim quickly ducked back to safety, still game, his desire to inflict damage on the enemy not in the least deterred by the perilous position he was in.

He tried once more, but once again bullets either slammed into the tree or split the air around him with angry whistling.

Blue Richards had been watching from nearby. "Forgit it, Kim," he hollered over. "They ain't no way yo're gonna use that M seventy-nine without makin' a target of yourself!"

"Bullshit!" Kim yelled. He tried again. This time he felt something slap his right deltoid muscle with the force of a karate kick. The M79 spun off one way and Kim the other. The Korean marine hit the ground but was not stunned enough to stay there in the exposed position which left him in full view of the enemy. He quickly rolled back to his foxhole and fumbled for his first aid kit, but found he couldn't use his right arm no matter how hard he tried.

"Medic!" Blue called out. "Kim's hit!"

Farther forward, Malpractice quickly slung his rifle across his back and slithered toward the rear, dragging his field medical bag with him.

Kim saw him coming. "Go back. I okay."

Malpractice ignored him and quickly snaked his way across a perilous open area until he slid into Kim's hole and ended up nearly on top of him.

"Let's have a look," Malpractice said.

"Hit in shoulder. Bone okay," Kim remarked with a grimace.

Malpractice quickly grasped the torn sleeve and ripped it open. Then he carefully inspected the wound. Most of the meat on the shoulder was blown away. A large, lightly bleeding cavern took the place of where once living muscle had been.

The injury was still numb, but Kim knew there would be plenty of pain within a half hour. But he grinned at the medic. "Not too bad, huh?"

"Naw," Malpractice replied in his best bedside manner, "but you'll be a coupla pounds lighter the next time you weigh yourself." The medic daubed the wound with a cleansing gauze to remove the dirt and other debris that Kim had picked up while crawling to is position. "I'm gonna shoot you up with lidocaine, Kim. Then I got to clean this thing out. What'd you do? Roll over here?"

"I think so," Kim said. "But I don't want nothing, okay? Got to stay alert to fight."

Malpractice snorted. "Suit yourself, tough guy. But whenever you decide you've had enough, let me know. I got to get to work on debridement—and I ain't got a operating room to do it in."

"What wrong with right here?" Kim asked.

"Only about ten thousand things," Malpractice said digging into his bag. He looked into Kim's eyes. "Here we go."

Kim nodded and grinned. "You the doctor."

"Whether you like it or not," Malpractice said. He ripped apart a sterile package and withdrew a pair of

198

surgical gloves. After giving Kim a reassuring wink, he slipped them on and went to work.

The medic gently probed the open injury, removing a couple of freshly formed blood clots and the rest of the foreign objects that had gotten in during the Korean marine's awkward and quick retreat back to his fighting hole.

"How it look now?" Kim asked.

"Lovely," Malpractice said. He made a careful inspection to check for any leaking blood vessels or nerve damage. Everything seemed fine, but the medic found some bone fragments. The round that hit Kim nicked the shoulder joint slightly, leaving a few splinters behind.

Kim got impatient. "Hey! How long this take, huh?"

"As long as I want it to," Malpractice replied. "Wounded people that crawl through the dirt have no business complainin' to hardworkin' medical personnel about the time it takes to clean 'em up." He turned his attention back to his bag and got a bottle. He liberally soaked the wound in physiologic salt solution. "I want you to pull out and head for the rear."

"No way," Kim said.

"Look," Malpractice said. "You're gonna be in shock pretty quick if you don't. This here thing you got'll need drainage and plenty of dressin' changes." He took a pair of scissors and quickly snipped at Kim's fatigue jacket, then removed the garment and tossed it aside. After that, he pulled a sterile bandage from his bag and carefully applied it to the wound. The next step involved applying a sling to keep Kim's arm immobile.

"I stay and fight!" Kim said angrily. "I—" He hesitated, then tried to speak again but couldn't.

Malpractice patted the Korean's good shoulder. "See what I mean?"

Kim closed his eyes and went into a quick deep breathing exercise. For several moments the *karateka* inhaled oxygen, but even his superb training couldn't help him. He started to go limp.

Malpractice knew he didn't have much time. He glanced out of the hole and took quick note of the combat. The fighting, which had flared up so quickly, had settled down to a roar as both sides now acted more logically. The first, heady excitement of the battle was gone.

"Well," Malpractice said to himself. "It's now or never." He slid his medical bag over his shoulder, then picked up Kim. After sliding out of the hole, the medic struggled to an upright position under the weight of his human burden.

The next order of business was to run like hell for the village that lay on the other side of the jungle.

Bullets zipped by, smacking into the vegetation, but Malpractice ignored them as he continued speeding deeper into the cover. The firing at him died down, then stopped completely. He slowed down to a trot in order to avoid jostling Kim too much. By the time he'd walked out of the brush into the open village, Kim had lost all consciousness.

"*Wai-shang-tui-ping!*" a feminine voice cried out.

Malpractice looked up to catch sight of one of the women that Tsang had given him. He grinned at her as she motioned for him to follow her through the hamlet to the jungle on the other side.

"We got *i-uen*," she said. "*I-uen?* You understand?"

"No," Malpractice answered. "But lead ahead. I'm willin' to go to this here *i-uen* if you want me to."

It only took them five minutes to reach a clearing. A camouflaged roof of palm fronds had been constructed and mounted above the opening in the jungle. The young woman pointed at it. "*I-uen!*"

Malpractice, still holding Kim in his arms, squatted down and looked inside. There were several injured women and children lying on small camp beds made of fronds. Now he understood the word. "Yes!" he said. "*I-uen*—hospital."

He took Kim to the back of the shelter and made him comfortable in an empty spot. After making sure his patient's legs were elevated, Malpractice once more turned to his medical bag for the things he needed. Within moments, he had mounted an intravenous bottle on a tree and had its Epinephrine slowly dripping down the rubber tube, through the needle into Kim's arm. This would keep the feisty Korean from going deeper into shock.

Malpractice motioned to the woman. "You watch him. Okay?"

She grinned, delighted she could be of some help. "Okay!"

Malpractice kissed her on the cheek. "You be good while I'm gone, huh?" The dedicated medic took one last look at his patient, then rushed back to the war.

KGB Lieutenant Colonel Krashchenko was deeply involved into his favorite pastime—paperwork.

The incoming reports from Major Dnang and his crack battalion of Viet Cong had given all indications that the destruction and/or capture of the Black Eagles was only a matter of time. That meant Krashchenko had nothing to do at all until the situation was resolved to his liking.

He decided to fill in those empty hours by taking out all his files and reading through the various cases. Such mundane activity could produce amazing results at times.

After having an extra table brought into the office, Krashchenko began to methodically sort out the various manila folders that held the intelligence he had gathered during his stay in North Vietnam. Mostly these were reports from situations created by Maj. Robert Mikhaelovich Falconi and his Black Eagles. But there were other cases there, too, some of which he had not worked on.

As Krashchenko studied and compared the data, he began to amass notes. Several rosters of enemy agents began to build up. He quickly checked these off against others he had. They always matched up together like a well-planned jigsaw puzzle—except for one particular area.

There was an enemy agent that he had dubbed *Neizvestnin Zhenshiya*—Unknown Woman.

This individual had been linked to the assassination of no less than three high-ranking personages in North Vietnam before mysteriously disappearing. There was no doubt it was the same woman. The description in all cases matched. Her method of operation was to appear in places where she could make contact with important personages. Then, using sex, she would neutralize the individual with gun, knife, or drugs. The subject was an Asian woman in her twenties, beautiful, and rather tall. In fact, she was taller than most Oriental men.

Somewhere, deep in Krashchenko's Slavic skull, a bell rang.

He went to the phone and dialed the communications room. When his call was answered, he spoke tersely. "Major Truong, quickly."

Within moments, Truong's voice came on the line. Once he had been feisty and disrespectful toward the Soviet officer before, but now the North Vietnam officer spoke in a humble manner, even using Russian as a courtesy. *"Da, Polkovnik* Krashchenko?"

"Get your little yellow ass up here *shivoi!"*

"Da, Polkovnik. Shivoi!"

It only took Truong three minutes to rush up the stairs from the basement and reach the office. He walked in and saluted.

Krashchenko tossed him the Black Eagles' roster he had been painstakingly making up for the previous few months. "Is that up to date?"

Truong nodded. "Yes. Except for the addition of the new members who joined Falconi after his Saigon operation."

"And the auxiliaries there? What are their names?"

"The CIA man Fagin and a South Vietnamese army woman lieutenant named Andrea Thuy," Truong said.

"Have you carefully noted her physical description?" Krashchenko asked.

Truong nodded. "Of course, comrade lieutenant colonel. She is tall and slim."

"Height and weight?"

"A bit over one and half meters tall and she weighs approximately fifty-four and a half kilograms, comrade lieutenant colonel," Truong answered. "This is information we garnered from the late ARVN Colonel Ngai."

Krashchenko tossed him the dossier on Unknown Woman. "Make a comparison."

Truong's quick eyes noted the physical description. He was amazed. "Why, comrade! It appears as if the Unknown Woman is none other than the administrative coordinator of the Black Eagles—Andrea Thuy!"

"Exactly," Krashchenko said. "Hasn't our agent Xong developed a new source of intelligence in that disgruntled South Vietnamese lieutenant named Trang?"

"The guard officer at MACV Headquarters? Yes, comrade," Truong replied.

"Have this verified as quickly as possible," Krashchenko said.

"*Da, Polkovnik!*"

Robert Falconi, with Archie Dobbs and Ray Swift Elk

behind him, continued their frantic trek toward the Ping village. Archie kept his commander heading in the right direction by hoarsely correcting his sometimes erratic path of travel.

"Half right, skipper! A little bit more! Yeah! That's it, but be careful. You keep wandering off to the left!"

Falconi hadn't abandoned noise discipline altogether, but he was certainly not giving it a lot of consideration. Limbs loudly whisked across their uniforms, and dried twigs cracked under their boots as the three pressed on to aid their comrades who were under both ground and air attack.

"*Ai do?*"

Falconi went to the ground. Archie and Swift Elk simultaneously followed his example.

The voice called out again. "*Ai do?*"

Falconi, flat on his belly, eased back to his companions. "Flank patrol," he whispered.

"Damn!" Archie hissed. "I knew we'd run into some o' the bastards before we reached the village."

The Viet Cong who had heard them became more insistent. "*Chuyen gi vay?*"

"He wants to know what's going on and who we are," Falconi said. "My accent sucks, but maybe I can draw 'em out."

"Then what?" Archie asked.

"As the old four hundred forty-second RCT used to say, 'Go for broke'!"

Swift Elk smirked. "And as my ancestors used to say, 'It's a good day to die'!"

Archie looked over and frowned at the Sioux. "Couldn't they think o' somethin' a little more cheerful than that?"

There was a rustle of bushes ahead. "*Ai do?*"

"*Toi day* Nguyen," Falconi answered with his mouth close to the ground to mask it as much as possible. He had

204

identified himself with a common Vietnamese name.

"Nguyen?" the unknown VC inquired. *"Con ai nua?"*

"Go!" Falconi said.

The three leaped to their feet and charged blindly in the direction of the voice. They pounded awkwardly through the jungle with the heavy stolen weapons slung on their backs. Their M16s, put on full auto for maximum firepower, chattered out short streams of bullets.

A couple of screams ahead showed they were going the right way. Falconi crashed into an opening and found himself facing a confused—but pissed off—Viet Cong officer. The man brought up his Chinese model of the Soviet M1933 pistol and fired point-blank at the Black Eagle's face.

Falconi felt a slap on the top of his head. His field cap was whisked away. Before the VC could shoot again, the major swung his rifle into a vertical butt stroke, driving the bottom of the stock into the Commie's chin. Falconi quickly brought the weapon back to the on-guard position, then lowered the muzzle and sent a blast into the writhing guerrilla officer. The Red did a beautiful twitching dance in the prone position on the jungle floor before finally rolling over in death.

"Wow! The funky chicken!" Falconi exclaimed before resuming his running charge. He crashed back into the dense vegetation.

"Skipper!" Archie's voice sounded off to his right.

"Yo!" the Falcon yelled back. He changed direction and caught up with the scout and Swift Elk.

Archie grinned. "I told you, skipper. You got a real bad tendency to wander off to your left."

"It's my Russian heritage," Falconi replied. "Let's get going again."

*   *   *

"Here they come again!" Top said into his radio. Proper voice procedure seemed rather innocuous at that point.

The rice paddies ahead of them suddenly sprouted hundreds of Viet Cong. The Reds surged toward the Black Eagle positions as the defensive fire built up.

Blue Richards and Charlie the Tripper were forced to take up the slack left by Kim's absence. Having been positioned on his flanks, they now had to extend the inner points of their fields of fire to make up for the loss. This meant a lighter defensive fusillade in the center of their area.

The enemy on the edges caught hell as usual, but the casualties were much less in the middle. Within minutes there was a buildup of forces there. These fanatical Reds pressed their advantage and closed in on the two Black Eagles.

A half dozen VC suddenly appeared to the immediate front and charged.

"Shift fire!" Blue yelled in alarm. "Center!"

The Tripper instinctively pulled his muzzle in that direction and cut loose. He knocked down two with his first burst, missed with his second, and hit another with the third squeeze of his trigger.

But the remaining three closed in on him.

The middle Viet Cong fired point-blank into the Tripper's face. The plump supply sergeant's features exploded as the simultaneous pounding of three 7.62 slugs flung him backward from his fighting hole.

Blue Richards, who had been distracted by another buildup of enemy to his right, turned his attention to the trio who had reached the Tripper's position. He took quick, accurate single shots that punched into the Reds. Two of them flipped over to the deck, but the last one only staggered backward a couple of steps with a wound in the fleshy part of his thigh.

"Damn!" Blue swore, "My pa'd really chew my ass for missin' at that range!" His next shot went between the eyes, and the guerrilla joined his comrades in death.

Blue made a quick survey of his situation and noted the ominous buildup to his immediate front. He picked up the radio he'd inherited from Kim. "Top, this is Bravo. Over."

"This is Top. Over."

"Ever'body's down but me and I'm pressed hard. Ol' Tripper's bought farm! I lost contact with our Pings. Over," Blue reported. Then he had to fling the radio down and kick out some swarms of bullets at the insistent enemy working their way toward him.

Top was also unable to continue communications. He turned to Tsang and Andrea nearby. "We're pulling back into the jungle."

Andrea, well aware of the deteriorating situation, fired a couple of shots, then asked, "Can we set up a fire-and-maneuver scheme?"

"No way," Top said. He grabbed the radio again. "Haul ass! Haul ass! To the other side of the village. Set up in the jungle."

All along the line, both Black Eagles and Pings immediately responded. Though most hadn't heard the message, they quickly surmised what was going on from the actions of their comrades.

The withdrawal was ragged but effective—and timely. At the moment the front line had broken up and retreated, flanking units of Viet Cong converged on the scene. The only thing they managed to do was become entangled with their own men involved in the frontal attack.

While the Reds bumped and even shot at each other for a few frantic moments, Top got his charges back through the village and set them up in the far edge in the jungle brush.

207

Once again, with Tsang and Andrea for company, he settled into a makeshift command post.

Tsang was happy. "VC attack all fucked up."

Andrea, eagerly scanning the ruined village for the first sight of charging Communists, impatiently fingered the trigger of her M16. "Where are those bastards?"

A sudden lull swept over them, the quietness as thunderous as a bomb explosion.

"They're probably reorganizing to continue the pressure," Top suggested.

"That'd give us time to do our own revamping, won't it?" Andrea asked.

"Hardly!" Top exclaimed. He pointed at the sky above the far treeline. "Look!"

The two helicopter gunships, weapons blazing, swept in from the tropical sky.

CHAPTER FIFTEEN

Top Gordon ducked deeper into his fighting hole as the atmosphere above the position turned to a thunderous concussion of machine gun fire combined with the roar of helicopter engines. Dirt and chunks of trees and brush spun through the air, much of it landing inside on him.

"Damn!" he said to himself. "I think those sons of bitches are pissed off at us."

There was a momentary respite until Malpractice McCorckel's voice sounded in the vacuum of stillness. "Here comes the motherfucker with the rockets!"

Scattered explosions danced in a straight line through the village and into the jungle where the Black Eagles and Pings had situated themselves only moments before. Stunning detonations rendered the close environment into a flaming, thundering hell. The roar of the aerial assault punished eardrums so badly the survivors could barely hear the screams of the casualties.

Top got onto his radio immediately. "Alpha report. Over."

"This is Alpha," Calvin Culpepper's voice came back. "My team's scattered, but none of the Black Eagles is down. We're losin' a mess o' Pings, though. Over."

"Roger, Alpha," Top said. "Bravo, report. Over."

"This is Bravo," Blue Richards said. "I'm all alone now, Top. They's a few o' them li'l ol' Chinamen around here, but they're takin' a awful poundin'. I ain't got much contact with 'em. Over."

Top sat the radio down. He looked over at Andrea. "What do you see over on your side?"

Andrea raised her head a bit and checked the immediate area near her. "Everybody's down and behind cover. A few managed to find holes like we did, most are using trees and depressions in the ground."

"Christ!" Top said. He waved to Tsang. "How're things over there?"

"Real bunch o' shit!" the Ping-Yan-Uen leader yelled back. "No much cover. Lotta mans go to the old generals."

Top nodded. "We might all be talking to those guys ourselves before the day's out."

Sounds of alarm echoed from the defensive line. Top looked up to see the helicopters coming in one more time. He hollered the oldest order in military history:

"Hit the dirt!"

The sound of the approaching engines increased until once again the entire world seemed to have deteriorated into one gigantic machine gun fusillade. Explosions, pounding slugs, and ricocheting bullets blended in with the violent ripping apart of the jungle. A couple of faint screams could barely be heard before the attacking chopper roared on over them.

And, as the last time, there was a few precious seconds of blissful silence before the rocket aircraft swooped in.

The series of explosions pounded like thundering sledgehammer blows. The force of the detonations hurled large hunks of village huts through the air as they slammed through the Ping's now nearly flattened hamlet. The orange flames of the rocket hits marched into the jungle like a trail of sprouting volcanoes. This time there was human debris, dismembered yet flailing, that careened into the sky, then fell back to earth with sickening thuds.

Top started to raise up but suddenly a weight crashed in on him. "Goddamn it!" he bellowed. He tried to untangle himself and find out what the hell was going on.

"Relax, Top," Falconi said. "As General MacArthur said, 'I have returned.'"

Top, despite his discomfort, was genuinely happy to see the Falcon. "When did you get back?"

"This very second, Top," Falconi answered.

"I'm glad to see you and all that, but how about getting the hell off me, skipper?" Top requested.

"Sorry," the Falcon remarked. He rolled away to the earth wall of the hole. "I didn't know if any more choppers were coming in or not. So I ran across the clearing and jumped in your command post here without bothering to make a formal announcement."

"No sweat, skipper. Did you get those machine guns?"

"Right. Where's Tsang?"

"I here, oh-you-kid," Tsang said. He'd crawled up to Top's hole after seeing Falconi jump in on top of the master sergeant. "You got guns?"

"Yeah. Where is that ammo?"

"Come! Come! It in cache where women and children hide."

Falconi crawled out of the position and followed the short Chinese into the jungle. He waved to Archie Dobbs and Ray Swift Elk who were waiting just inside the treeline. "Let's go. We have to be ready for those choppers when they come back."

Archie glanced skyward. "We'll never make it."

"Remember the old Sioux saying," Swift Elk reminded him as they rushed after their commander. "It's a good day to die!"

Lt. Trang Loc, dressed in an expensive civilian suit,

strolled casually into the Caravel Bar in downtown Saigon. The luxurious attire had also been a "gift" from the dry cleaning driver for information he had been supplying from his job as officer of the guard at MAC V Headquarters.

The ARVN stopped and glanced around until he caught sight of a Vietnamese, also well dressed, sitting in a booth along the back wall. The man had a red handkerchief sticking from his jacket pocket. Trang walked up to him and nodded. "*Chao ong.* You look familiar to me. Have you ever been in Xin Loc?"

"No. But I have an uncle there," the stranger, who appeared to be a businessman, replied.

"Is his name Hoa?"

"Yes."

Trang slid into the booth opposite the other man. The casual conversation was a carefully planned password and recognition signal. The night before, with the delivery of his dry cleaning and money, the driver Xong—code named Bua—had set Trang up for this particular meeting.

The Vietnamese officer offered his hand. "I am Trang."

"Of course. You may call me Ngoc."

A waiter appeared and took Trang's order of a Dewer and soda with a twist. Thanks to the extra income he now earned, the lieutenant was now able to partake of the better brands of his favorite drink. He and Ngoc conversed casually and in low tones until the barman reappeared and sat Trang's glass down.

"What is it you wish of me, Mr. Ngoc?"

"We need information on a certain person in MAC V Headquarters," Ngoc said. "And, if you are able to get it, there will be a handsome bonus for you."

"*Duoc roi!* Who is this person?"

"Andrea Thuy," Ngoc replied. "Do you know her?"

212

"Very well," Trang answered. "She is out with the Black Eagle detachment at this very moment."

Ngoc almost spilled his drink. *"Cai do la cai gi?* Are you sure?"

"Of course," Trang said. "Bua ordered me to give the Black Eagles all my attention. Therefore, I have made myself present at all briefings and conferences."

"Most interesting!" Ngoc said. "We need a dossier on her, including recent photographs. Can you get one?"

"I'm not sure," Trang said. "All personnel files pertaining to Black Eagle operations are kept in a special safe. However, I have learned many things about her over the long months I have served at MAC V. For example, she is a Eurasian."

Ngoc leaned forward. "Yes? Yes? Go on!"

"Her father was a French missionary doctor and her mother a Vietnamese nurse," Trang continued. "They were killed by the Viet Minh quite a long time ago."

"She is illegitimate?"

"No," Trang said. "Her parents were married."

"Thuy is not a French name," Ngoc reminded him. "If her parents were man and wife, she would be using her father's name."

"True," Trang said. "After her parents were killed, she was taken to a Catholic orphanage by French paras. She was only an infant and could not say her last name. Thuy was given her by the nuns that took her in. Andrea Thuy is actually Andrea Roget."

"Roget," Ngoc said. "Ah! That will help us fill in any gaps you may leave out."

"Am I to understand this is of primary importance?"

"Yes!" Ngoc said. "We shall expect a report without delay, then continue to supply us with information as often as you possibly can."

"Will this be done through you or the driver?"

"Through me," Ngoc replied. "You and I shall become

213

very good *friends*, Lieutenant Trang. We shall meet for drinks often and attend sporting events together. You may speak of me openly with your colleagues in the army. By the way, do you play golf?"

"No," Trang answered. "I've never been closely associated with that crowd."

Ngoc smiled. "Your lifestyle is about to change. In fact, next Sunday you and I shall go out to the Xin Loc Country Club and I will introduce you to the game."

Trang lit a cigarette. "I shall have to rearrange my schedule to meet all these demands."

"See that you do," Ngoc said. "You may go now."

Trang finished his drink. "Of course." He stood up and bowed slightly to Ngoc, then spoke loud enough to be heard. "If I am ever in Xin Loc I shall say hello to your uncle. And thank you for the invitation to play golf Sunday. I shall look forward to it. *Chao ong*."

Ngoc nodded his head. *"Chao ong."*

Trang walked rapidly to the door, his mind already filling with ideas of how to accomplish this latest request on revealing Andrea Thuy *née* Roget to the Communists.

Capt. Bohumir Sprosty kicked a hard right rudder and wheeled his aircraft through the sky. Grinning, he grabbed the microphone. *"Podporupcik Somad, Jak se dari?"*

Young Lieutenant Somad's voice came through the earphones, "I have enough ammunition left for one more run."

"Dobre! So do I, comrade. Let us strafe the capitalist gangsters one more time, then return to reload."

"Ano, kapitan!"

Sprosty continued the wide turn through the air until he was once again lined up for the run. So far this whole

214

episode had been a piece of cake. He couldn't understand the old veterans when they would talk of being frightened during the fighting against the Germans during World War II. Combat was fun! All that was required was to fly one's helicopter at the enemy and shoot them up.

He cranked the throttle while lowering the collective. The helicopter streaked in toward the target area. Sprosty, grinning, shouted aloud, "*Bavim se velmi dobre!*"

His finger rested slightly on the firing button, ready to apply more pressure at the exact moment the quad-Goryunov machine gun barrels were in proper alignment.

The jungle, only a few meters below, zoomed underneath the chopper. Sprosty could see his Viet Cong comrades on the ground looking up at him from the rice paddies. Then the village came into view. He began to tighten his finger—

The cockpit glass exploded in on him and 7.62 millimeter slugs punched into his chest, exploding out the Czech's back to continue through the seat and the rear bulkhead into the troop compartment. Sprosty's hands and feet left the controls as he slumped over to one side.

The MI-4 helicopter, now flying itself, slowed up and gently turned, going into an ever widening circle.

Chuck Fagin stepped into the conference room. He was surprised to see Lieutenant Trang seated at the officer of the guard's desk by the door. He smiled at the ARVN officer. "Hello, Trang. I thought this was your day off."

Trang shook his head. "I haven't been real satisfied with the men lately," he explained. "In fact, I was worrying about it so much, I decided to report in for duty. It seemed a waste of time to be out on the town and not able to enjoy it."

"You're a real eager beaver," Fagin said. "That's good, but you've got to learn to delegate authority."

Trang laughed. "What's that old American saying about if you want something done right, do it yourself?"

"That's it," Fagin said. He patted Trang on the shoulder. "You keep this up and you'll be a general in six months."

Trang smiled bitterly. "Perhaps." Then he changed the subject. "What are you doing here? Is there a special meeting?" The officer already knew the answer to that one. He had seen it scheduled on the operations roster.

"Yes. I've called in Clayton Andrews. Do you remember him?"

"Sure!" Trang said. "I recall when he had the job you are now doing."

"He's my boss now, and I'm going to badger the hell out of him," Fagin said.

"What about?"

"Falconi and—" He stopped speaking as the door opened. "You're just about to find out."

Clayton Andrews, the senior CIA case officer for Special Operations Group of MAC V, stepped into the room. A couple of American colonels and a Vietnamese brigadier general were with him. He walked over to Fagin. "Here I am, as per your request."

"Hello, Mr. Andrews," Trang said.

Andrews turned and looked at the ARVN officer, "I'll be damned! You still here, Trang? I figured you'd be leading a division by now."

Trang shook his head. "Afraid not. I'm still in charge of local security, as always."

"Then there's nothing to worry about around this place," Andrews said. "Let's talk later."

"Sure, Mr. Andrews."

Andrews and Fagin walked over to a conference table where the officers who had come in with the senior CIA

216

man were introduced. Fagin learned that these particular men had been detailed to command Operational Area Bravo as soon as it was neutralized by the Black Eagles and the Ping-Yan-Uen.

"Well," Fagin said. "You've seen the reports, so you know there's a big mystery involved there. Nobody knows if Falconi and his bunch are dead or alive—or prisoners."

Andrews shrugged and grinned. "You know the Falcon, for Chrissake! He likes to get off by himself and do his own thing without a bunch of interference from us paper pushers."

"There's been no commo for over eighty hours," Fagin protested. "He'd at least check in, wouldn't he?"

"He's probably lost his radio, or the damned thing isn't working," Andrews said unconcerned. Then he laughed. "Or that crazy sonofabitch threw it away so we wouldn't be bugging him."

"I don't think so," Fagin countered. "There's something wrong—dead wrong."

"Okay," Andrews conceded reluctantly. "What do you want us to do about it?"

"Let's put in a battalion," Fagin suggested. "Maybe some of those ass-kickers out of the One hundred first Airborne."

One of the American generals shook his head. "No way. We've got other commitments."

"Okay then!" Fagin shouted. "The One hundred seventy-third or the First Infantry—anybody, for God's sake!"

"We can't put line units into a hot area like that," Andrews said. "If Falconi's wasted, it would be like our guys riding choppers into downtown Hanoi. They wouldn't stand a chance."

"Then what the hell do you want to do?" Fagin asked. "Sit back and just wait to see what happens?"

"I'll tell you what," Andrews said. "Let's wait another seventy-two hours before we take action."

Fagin's face was a mask of anger. "If Falconi and his boys buy the farm, I'll have your ass, Andy."

"Now, now, Chuck!"

"I mean it, goddamn it! I'll hang you from the tallest flagpole at Langley."

Andrews sighed. "Okay! Okay! Back down a bit. I tell you what. I'll send an aerial reconnaissance over Operational Area Bravo."

"When?"

"In seventy-two hours."

"Bullshit! Tomorrow," Fagin insisted. "And make sure the pilot knows the frequency of Falconi's Prick-Six crystals. I have an idea that his big radio is inoperable. That's the one thing I'll agree with you on."

"Okay," Andrews said. He checked his watch. "I have another meeting in a few minutes. I'll set up the flight and get back with you." He walked to the door with the officers following him. The senior CIA man shook hands with Trang. "Nice seeing you again. Why don't we get together for a drink? Maybe Sunday. I'll have the day off."

"Sorry," Trang said. "I have a date to play golf."

"Golf?" Andrews inquired with a laugh. "Say! You're starting to move into the upper circles of society now, aren't you?"

"It seems so," Trang remarked.

"Well, we'll get together some other time," Andrews said. "I'd really like to renew our friendship."

"Same here, Mr. Andrews," Trang said holding the door open for him and the others. After they left, he turned to Fagin. "I'll see you later, Chuck. I think I'll go into town anyhow. Like you said—I should learn to delegate authority."

Fagin nodded a silent good-bye, then settled thoughtfully into a nearby chair.

Youthful Lieutenant Somad was confused.

His commanding officer, Captain Sprosty, had been leading him in on another aerial attack against the capitalist gangsters, when the captain's helicopter had suddenly shuddered violently and then gone into a graceful, slow turning maneuver.

Somad had never been trained to display any individualistic tendencies. Raised and educated in the Czechoslovak Socialist Republic, he had learned that such things as being too opinionated, headstrong, or uncooperative could result in various punishments ranging from corporal punishment for school children to imprisonment for adults. Therefore, when his commander suddenly went into the puzzling and purposeless flight, Somad did not question why. He simply followed as a good Communist was trained to do.

For a full twenty minutes the two helicopters orbited in a wide, lazy circle over the treetops. Their altitudes gradually lowered until Lieutenant Somad began to worry. In fact, he became so worried, he decided to ask his commander what the hell was going on. He picked up his microphone, hesitated, then spoke politely.

"*Kapitan* Sprosty, this is *Podporucik* Somad. Where are we going, sir?"

There was no answer as Sprosty's aircraft descended another few meters.

"*Kapitan* Sprosty? When are we going in for the next attack? We both have enough ammunition for one more before we must return to load."

Again there was silence. But they were now so low the young lieutenant could see the prop wash of Sprosty's chopper blowing leaves from the tops of trees. He wisely eased up on his throttle to put more distance between himself and the other helicopter.

"*Kapitan* Sprosty, I still have rockets left," he said. Then he inquired, "Why are we flying at this altitude?"

Now Sprosty's wheels were hitting the top branches of the jungle, sending hunks of fronds hurtling backward.

"I advise immediate ascent, *Kapitan* Sprosty!" Somad hung on doggedly until the instinct of survival finally overrode his instinct to be a good little Commie. He pulled up on the collective and gained altitude. "*Kapitan* Sprosty? *Kapitan* Sprosty! Pull up! Pull up!"

Sprosty's Chinese built MI-4 Helicopter hit the tops of the trees and tipped forward violently. Then it simply disappeared into the jungle.

Somad banked sharply, then looked down to see a gaping hole where his commander had gone in. Suddenly the air was rent by an explosion and debris shot out of the jungle canopy like grapeshot from a cannon. The concussion rocked Somad's chopper, and he had to fight like hell to hang on.

Now the young lieutenant was completely confused. He didn't know why Sprosty had crashed, and he didn't know what was expected of him. His mind frantically sifted through what had just occurred, trying to reach some sort of a decision. His last orders had been to follow Sprosty to the attack. He had done exactly that, but now the captain had crashed. The other part of the orders now must be obeyed, he decided, so he turned back toward the village to carry them out by making a final attack before flying back to the base.

Somad could see the Viet Cong fighters below looking up at him as he zoomed over their position. He happily noted that some waved, and he knew they would be cheering him.

The village loomed up in his rocket sights, and he

prepared to press the firing button and send another swarm of rockets into the target.

But suddenly he was inundated by a hot, roaring flash. And, just as abruptly, he was out of it.

But something was definitely wrong.

Stunned and confused, he groped for his controls but could not find them. He felt his safety belt still holding him snug and secure in the seat, but things were horribly out of kilter. A sickening wave of dizziness held him in a tight, nauseating grip. A puzzling, but persistent wind whistled in his face, and he found it extremely difficult to focus his eyes on any one particular point.

Then he knew what had happened.

He was in his seat, all right, but the helicopter had gone off somewhere else on its own. His ship had been hit, and he'd been blown free of it.

The ground and sky whizzed past his vision as he somersaulted through the tropical sky and finally crashed through the trees, the force of the impact ripping him from the aircraft seat and pancaking him against the gnarled roots of an ancient *ho* tree.

Archie Dobbs sat the Red Chinese type 53 machine gun back on the ground. He and Swift Elk glanced at each other and winked their mutual congratulations after the second chopper had been blown from the sky.

"Nice shootin', Redskin," Archie said in an exaggerated cowboy accent.

"Not too bad yourself, White-eyes," Swift Elk replied. Then he patted the automatic weapon. "If my dear old grandpa had carried one o' these at the Little Big Horn, he wouldn't have stopped at Custer."

221

CHAPTER SIXTEEN

M.Sgt. Chun Kim of the Republic of Korea Marine Corps was a *karateka*. In fact, he held a third degree black belt in the Tai Kwon Do discipline of karate.

To the uninitiated, this meant he was an expert in hand-to-hand combat and able to employ this martial art to his own best advantage in fights. This was true, of course, but the art of karate goes much deeper than breaking other people's noses or shattering their bones with lethal punches and kicks.

Karate is also a spiritual exercise. The properly trained and indoctrinated devotee is able to apply the mental aspects of the discipline in conjunction with the physical ones. Any student who is unable to maintain the proper mental attitudes and strengths could never reach the ranks of black belt. Instead, he would only struggle along in the *dojo*, a serious source of embarrassment to his teacher.

The basic reason for this mind-over-matter aspect is to galvanize the physical actions with those of the deep psyche. But a man like Kim, after long years of deep, steady practice as a *karateka* is able to take this meditative quality a few steps farther.

He could control his body's functions to the nth degree.

The bullet that hit the Korean marine did massive damage to his shoulder. A large hunk of deltoid muscle was gouged out, leaving a gaping cavity. While not necessarily fatal during the primary moments of injury, this type of wound can eventually kill through shock. When Kim was struck by the round, he was not in the peak of physical condition. He had been in continuous combat for several days; he hadn't eaten well nor had he rested, and his mind was clouded with the responsibilities of being in command of a fire team.

He had gone into shock, and the medic Malpractice McCorckel had treated him in the proper manner by taking him to a quieter area and injecting him with the proper drugs.

Kim's body slept, but his mind leaped into action. Although unconscious, he delved deep into the innermost recesses of his mental processes and summoned forth the strength to instruct his flesh what it was to do to heal itself. This accelerated the normal activity of the physique during illness and injury, so Kim's psychic energy began doing what the most modern drugs and medicines never could.

By the time the two helicopters had been shot down and the defense line reorganized for the addition of the machine guns, Kim had not only pulled the intravenous device out of his arm, he was sitting up and wanting to get back into action.

Falconi went to the crude jungle hospital to visit him and was surprised at the Korean's condition. "Damn, Kim! Malpractice said you were down for the count."

"I'm okay, skipper," Kim said in his heavy accent. "A little sore—that's all. Ready to fight, okay?"

"Sure," Falconi said. "I heard your grenade launcher was blown to hell."

"Yeah. Really piss me off too," Kim said.

Falconi studied the team leader closely, noting his

right arm was still in a sling. Then he swung the commando mortar off his shoulder and showed it to him. "Know what this is?"

Kim grinned. "Sure! Is little mortar."

"Think you can fire it?"

"You bet, skipper!"

"How do you know? You've never seen it work before."

"I can still fire it," Kim insisted.

"Okay," Falconi said. "Let's try it with a simulation, huh? Grab the tube with your right hand."

Kim did so and was able to hold on and swing the weapon back and forth within the limits of the sling. "How that, skipper?"

"Pretty good," Falconi answered. "As a matter of fact, that sling gives you a steadier hold on the thing. Keeps it from wobbling."

"Sure, skipper. Now what?"

"Pretend to drop a round down the tube with your left hand, then pull the lanyard."

"Okay." Kim dropped an imaginary shell into the mortar. Then he grabbed the lanyard and pulled it. "Boom!" he said laughing.

Falconi chuckled too. "Well! It looks like our mortar crew is organized and functioning."

"You bet, skipper!" Kim said happily. "Bring on VC motherfucker!"

Lt.Col. Gregori Krashchenko and Maj. Truong Van had temporarily forgotten their feud.

This wasn't because of any growing affection between them, but rather because of the man who now sat insolently at Krashchenko's own desk.

This individual's name was Vlademir Kuznetz. Although he had been in Hanoi for several years, this was one Russian who was an almost total unknown. He wasn't a shy man by any stretch of the imagination, but he craved anonymity. This was because of his job as the senior ranking KGB man in Southeast Asia.

Now, a glass of Krashchenko's vodka in front of him—and his personal aide behind—this fat, heavily browed guardian of Communism fairly bubbled with joy. He picked up the drink and noisily sucked some into his mouth before swallowing it. He grinned at Krashchenko. "You did a *prichudpivi* job, comrade."

"*Spasibo*," Krashchenko said thanking him for the compliment.

"As of this moment, we have that Falconi and his men bottled up, just waiting for us to put the stopper in," Kuznetz said. "Like catching a bunch of moths, hey?" He looked around at his aide. "That's what it's like, right, Pivrenyeh?"

"*Da*, comrade general," Pivrenyeh quickly and correctly answered.

Krashchenko enjoyed the look of anguish on Truong's face. He turned to Kuznetz. "Now, there is nothing left to do but let our Viet Cong comrades slowly close the noose around Falconi's neck."

"*Medlenieh*—slowly?" the KGB general said. "*Nyet!* We are going to charge the swine and swallow him up."

Krashchenko felt misgivings. "But, comrade general, wouldn't it be better to close off all exits and move against him and his men in a deliberate manner?"

"What for?" Kuznetz asked. "We have him outnumbered, outgunned, and completely at our mercy. We shall have Comrade Major Dnang order his men to the final attack."

Krashchenko was now nervous. "May I offer a suggestion, comrade general?"

"What is that?"

"That you reconsider your plan," Krashchenko said.

"We have had Falconi and his men in similar situations before. Rash acts have proven unwise and—"

"Rash acts!" Kuznetz thundered. "You consider my tactical decisions as rash acts?"

"Of course not, comrade general, but—"

"Do you fear Falconi? Do you think of him as some sort of a superman?"

"Nyet, tovarisch general!"

"Then I want my orders followed immediately," Kuznetz insisted. "Without further comments from you." He turned to Truong. "Transmit the battle instructions."

"Wait!" Krashchenko exclaimed. He swallowed nervously. "I must—must, with all respect, of course—I must protest your plans."

"You dare to protest?" Kuznetz shouted. "What do you think this is? The American Congress or British Parliament?"

"Of course not, comrade general, but—" Krashchenko felt great misgivings, but he went on anyway. "I wish to go on record as being against this plan."

"Really?" Kuznetz laughed, turning to his side. "Pivrenyeh, make a note of the date and time and write down that Comrade Lieutenant Colonel Krashchenko disagrees with my final orders to attack Major Falconi and the Black Eagles."

"May I have a copy?" Krashchenko asked timidly.

"Give him one," Kuznetz said. Then he turned to Truong and bellowed, "I thought I gave you an order! Go to your communications room and notify Comrade Major Dnang to attack Falconi and his bandits immediately, with everything they have. I want that capitalist swine crushed and his head brought to me!"

*   *   *

Maj. Dnang Quong, commander of the specially assembled Viet Cong Battalion, took his binoculars and scanned the sky. "Where are those helicopters?"

His adjutant Lieutenant Trun could only shrug. "I do not know, comrade major. We've heard two explosions. Perhaps they crashed."

"How?" Dnang demanded. "There are no anti-aircraft weapons over there. They have been making their attacks unopposed since this battle started. Have any of our men reported seeing the aircraft go down?"

"No, comrade major," Trun answered. "But it is possible for them to have crashed out of our view."

Dnang started to say more but stopped when he noted the radio operator near him taking down a message. He pointed at the communications man. "That is probably the helicopter captain now. Perhaps he had to refuel or get more ammunition."

"Yes, comrade major," Trun answered.

They waited until the man finished writing down the signals he was receiving. The soldier took off his earphones and handed the slip of paper to Dnang.

Trun licked his lips in anticipation. "What is it, comrade major? Are the Czechoslovakians flying back to give us more air support?"

Dnang shook his head. "No. These are orders telling us to launch a massive, decisive attack without delay."

Trun smiled. "*Murng ong*, comrade major! Your time of glory has arrived. We will score a great victory without the East European comrades."

Dnang shrugged. "I do not know if it will be considered a great victory. The Black Eagles and their mercenary friends are without heavy support weapons. We shall simply crush them."

"*Co*, comrade major!"

"Order the platoon leaders to launch the assault immediately."

CHAPTER SEVENTEEN

The sounds of distant whistles came from the area of the rice paddies.

"That'll be the VC squad and platoon leaders alerting their men," Top explained to Falconi.

"They'll be hitting us anytime," Falconi said.

"Are you going to fire any rounds to zero in the mortar?" Top asked.

"I'm afraid not," Falconi answered. "In the first place, we don't have enough ammo for the thing to waste any. And, since it's aimed and fired by hand, there's no guarantee that any zeroing in will be effective anyhow. Then there's also the reason that I don't want those sons of bitches to know we have the damned thing."

A rolling crescendo of small arms' fire broke out along the line. Falconi's radio sprang to life with Archie Dobbs's voice. The point man had set himself up in an observation post a hundred meters in front of the defensive line.

"Falcon, this is Scout. Charlie is coming at us. Over."

"Roger, Scout," Falconi replied. "Leave your position and fall back to the main line of resistance. Over."

"Roger. Out."

Ray Swift Elk, manning one of the Chinese machine

guns, had Calvin Culpepper covering his exposed flank. He waved over at the black sergeant. "Keep a good eye out in that direction, Buffalo Soljer."

"You got it, Injun," Calvin yelled back.

A skirmish line of VC burst through the vegetation on the other side of the village and charged toward their positions. Swift Elk pulled the charging handle back and let it slam home into battery. Then he began to fire the 7.62 automatic weapon like he was playing a pipe organ.

The Sioux was a virtuoso on his instrument. Long, accurate streams of steel-jacketed slugs played out of the muzzle, sweeping back and forth along the enemy ranks. The VC staggered, spun, and collapsed in those unexpected volleys of fire.

"Right on, Injun!" Calvin yelled. He pumped methodic, well-aimed shots into the far area that Swift Elk couldn't cover. His own firing hammered into the attacking Reds with deadly persistence. The Viet Cong held up as their casualties mounted, but only for a moment. Then they once again put on the pressure, trying to move through the hail of steel the two Black Eagles threw out in front of them.

Blue Richards had fixed himself up in a camouflaged position that would do credit to any duck blind in Alabama. Blended in well with the surroundings, he took advantage of his near invisibility to do what he did best with a rifle. Shoot single, well-aimed, accurate shots.

A confused Red, seeing a couple of his buddies catch headshots and pitch over, squatted down and stared ahead of him to see who had done the damage.

Blue took a deep breath and slowly exhaled as he simultaneously increased the pressure on the trigger and set the sights on the Viet Cong's head.

The M16 kicked back slightly into his shoulder as it fired. The bullet zipped across the space and punched into the Red's forehead. The skull exploded out the back, flipping the scalp over to cover the man's face. He sat down, his feet drumming on the ground in the throes of death, before toppling over to lie quietly and sweetly on the ground.

Bullhorn Maywood, assigned to cover Archie Dobbs on the other machine gun, found the work demanding. He had already run two complete magazines through his weapon and had just crammed the third in while the pressure on that part of the line kept building. "Give 'em more on the flanks!" he yelled at Archie.

"Gotcha!" Archie responded. He swung the muzzle over and cut loose with telling shots that spilled five VC to the ground in bloody heaps.

"This is a mass attack!" Bullhorn complained.

"Don't worry!" Archie yelled between shots. "The skipper'll be bringin' in that mortar anytime now."

Back in the rear, with his radio volume turned all the way up, Chun Kim sat in eager readiness. The shells were stacked neatly on his left, and he held the commando mortar tightly with his right hand.

Falconi's voice came out of the Prick-Six's receiver. "This is Falcon. Fire three rounds for effect. Over."

Holding the tube with a slight lean forward, Kim picked up a round and dropped it into the weapon's muzzle. Then he gently pulled the lanyard. The little monster coughed out the round with a loud report.

Kim quickly fired two more and waited.

Within seconds he heard the three explosions. Falconi came over the air again. "You gotta drop back. You overshot the area. Try three more."

Kim pulled the tube more erect and cut loose with another trio of the deadly shells. This time the detonations sounded closer.

"Right on, Kim! Give 'em hell!"

Grinning viciously, Kim began to methodically operate the mortar. He spaced the shots five seconds apart,

231

moving the muzzle slightly each time to increase the field of coverage.

Back with Archie, Bullhorn Maywood whooped his joy as the small explosion erupted in front, throwing VC into the air or blowing them sideways like they'd been hit by hurricane-force winds.

"Way to go, Kim! Way to go, baby!" he hollered. He flipped the M16 to full auto and hosed the front area as the pressure from the VC lessened somewhat.

But he didn't see the wounded guerrilla only twenty meters away. The man, hiding behind a dead comrade, had propped his AK47 on the body. He aimed carefully and fired.

Bullhorn, kneeling behind a tree, caught the bullet in the right eye. He spun completely around and flopped over on his back, his mangled features looking up at the dense canopy of jungle overhead.

"You sonofabitch!" Archie Dobbs screamed in rage. He pushed the Chinese machine gun around and cut loose with one long burst. The bullets hammered into the Viet Cong sniper, picking him up and rolling him along the ground like a rag doll until Archie finally eased up on the trigger.

The scout turned his attention back to his field of fire and noted the pressure had lessened considerably. He angrily and quickly scanned the front of the combat lines but could see nothing.

"C'mon, you sonofabitches!" Archie bellowed in rage.

But the fighting had died off altogether.

Maj. Dnang Quong crouched in the heavily overgrown gully, trying to catch his breath. A few meters to the front, among the dead and mangled of his battalion, the energetic Lieutenant Trun was finally still. A bullet, either from a Black Eagle or a Ping-Yan-Uen, had gouged out his throat. The young VC officer had died a horrible, painful death as he coughed and strangled in his own blood.

Dnang couldn't understand what had happened to the tactical situation. Only a few hours before, he and his men had been enjoying tactical superiority with helicopter gunship support. The enemy had been unable to put up a real effective defense. They had lasted as long as they did from the necessity of Dnang and his men having to attack across some exposed rice paddies. They had taken plenty of casualties, but that was no worry. Eventually, the Viet Cong would win as they pressed in closer to the Ping-Yan-Uen village.

Then everything went straight to hell.

The helicopters had dropped out of sight. True, only two had disappeared, but there was no way that Dnang could contact the others. Their radios and his field commo gear did not match up. Then the enemy suddenly opened up in the middle of things with machine gun and mortar support.

Dnang wiped at the sweat on his brow, leaving a muddy streak across his skin. He had undeniable orders to press the attack, and the major was not the sort to ever disobey. He took one deep breath and pulled the Tokarev pistol from the holster. "Comrades!" he yelled. "As skirmishers! Attack!"

There were weak yells along the Viet Cong line as the Reds moved out to once again assault the stubborn demons who doggedly held on to their defensive positions.

Dnang, holding his pistol ready, crashed through the brush until he reached the ruined village. He jumped and dodged through the debris of the smashed huts. The air around him now buzzed with flying bullets as he closed in toward the enemy.

He leaped over a line of his own dead and charged

forward. The Viet Cong major caught sight of a tall American, and instinct told him that this was the infamous Falconi. Dnang screamed in rage and raised his pistol. He fired frantically at the big man but missed.

Then suddenly a series of mortar rounds went off. The concussion threw Dnang through the air. He hit the ground painfully but managed to roll over and pull himself back to his feet.

At that moment he knew the battle was lost.

The stupid orders making his men attempt an all-out assault had proved their undoing. He took another look for Falconi. Then the bullets hit him in the stomach and chest. Dnang's head slammed hard against the hard-packed dirt of the village square. He tried to see what was going on but could only make out the hazy forms of enemy troops—American and Oriental—charging toward him and his men.

The last words he heard before he died were shrilled in exaltation:

"Gaaung-Po! Gaaung-Po!"

EPILOGUE

Maj. Robert Falconi and the rest of the Black Eagles stood beside what had been the rice paddies they'd used for a drop zone on their infiltration into the operational area.

The fight with the Viet Cong battalion had ended forty-eight hours previously. But U.S. Army engineers and their equipment had already been flown in on huge transport helicopters. They had immediately begun bulldozing and filling in the large area. Now it was a perfectly flat and solid landing field, capable of supporting the heaviest vehicles or weaponry. Even at that moment, a large Model S30 MB scraper worked the outer edges of the new terrain, putting on the finishing touches.

Several American units, mostly artillery and supporting infantry, were already established in a temporary fire base that they would use until the permanent setup was completed. Bunkers and 155 millimeter howitzers were ready for action.

Falconi glanced over at the jungle where the Pings were busy burying the dead VC in a mass grave. The Black Eagle commander slowly shook his head in wonder. "I'll never figure out what made them launch that last, stupid attack."

Top Gordon lit a cigarette. "If they'd called in more of those chopper gunships to soften us up with a few extra runs, they'd eventually gotten us," he admitted. "We couldn't have held them forever."

"I was sure glad to hear the liaison pilot's voice come over the Prick-Six," Falconi said. "That proved Chuck Fagin hadn't forgotten us."

"He never would," Andrea said.

"It would still have been too late for us if the VC hadn't gotten so impatient," Top interjected. "Those two machine guns and that little mortar wouldn't have assured us victory—only a delay of inevitable defeat."

"The only thing I can figure is that the Viet Cong commander received orders to do what he did," Falconi said. "He was doing a good job directing his people against us. It doesn't make sense that he'd suddenly turn stupid."

Andrea laughed. "Well, whoever told him to make an all-out attack is in big trouble right now." She started to say more but noted some people approaching from the Ping village. "Here comes Tsang and some of his men."

"Prob'ly wants to say good-bye," Archie Dobbs said. "You gotta admit we done a good job together."

"And paid a price," Ray Swift Elk said. He looked over at the poncho-shrouded bodies of Charlie Tripper and Bullhorn Maywood. "Too bad there wasn't enough left o' Sparks to take back."

"Yeah," Calvin Culpepper said. "Or that we had to leave poor ol' Toby Barker back in VC territory."

"I talked with the commander who came in with these new troops," Falconi said. "He said his guys would go out and police up the body."

Blue Richards looked up into the pale, steaming tropical sky. "Dead folks don't last long in weather like this. All they'll find is a pile o' bones."

"Oh-you-kid!" hollered Tsang. "You make ready to leave?"

"Yes," Falconi yelled back. He waited for the Ping captain and his men to approach.

Tsang had brought an honor guard with him. He quickly formed them up and presented arms. The Black Eagles, not to be outdone in military protocol, also fell in. Falconi returned the salute.

"*Toh-tse, Shiu-Kaau* Falconi," Tsang said, offering his hand. "It was a privilege to fight at your side."

"I feel the same," Falconi said in sincerity.

Tsang looked at Andrea. "And thanks to you, too, Sai-Chin-Sza-Tung—little Warrior-Sister."

"I am pleased to have brought you blessings," Andrea said.

"Are you and your men ready for your new role with the Americans who have just arrived?" Falconi asked.

"Yes, *Shiu-Kaau*," Tsang replied. "We are to be issued full complements of uniforms, helmets, weapons, and other equipment. It will be our job to provide patrols into the surrounding jungle to keep this new fire base secure. We are most happy."

The sudden beating of gigantic helicopter rotors sounded faintly in the background. Falconi turned toward it and looked until he made out the CH-21C Shawnee approaching. "Our ride home." He turned to Tsang. "Good-bye, friend."

"*Tsoi-kin,*" Tsang said.

The big chopper came in scattering dust as it settled onto the newly constructed landing zone. Falconi watched as the two dead Black Eagles were placed aboard. Then, after the rest of the detachment was aboard, he waved one more time at Tsang and joined them.

The gigantic aircraft pulled itself skyward, and the Falcon studied the ground during the ascent. From that altitude it was easy to see the many changes on the ground. What had been a simple village and abandoned rice paddies was now a large, fortified complex. Falconi glanced at the two bodies, then back down at the tiny figures of the soldiers toiling below.

"Make it worth it, guys," he said as the Shawnee banked and turned south toward Saigon where Chuck Fagin waited for them.

McLEANE'S RANGERS
by John Darby

#1: BOUGAINVILLE BREAKOUT   (1207, $2.50)
Even the Marines call on McLeane's Rangers, the toughest, meanest, and best fighting unit in the Pacific. Their first adventure pits the Rangers against the entire Japanese garrison in Bougainville. The target—an ammo depot invulnerable to American air attack . . . and the release of a spy.

#2: TARGET RABAUL   (1271, $2.50)
Rabaul—it was one of the keys to the control of the Pacific and the Japanese had a lock on it. When nothing else worked, the Allies called on their most formidable weapon—McLeane's Rangers, the fearless jungle fighters who didn't know the meaning of the word quit!

#3: HELL ON HILL 457   (1343, $2.50)
McLeane and his men make a daring parachute drop in the middle of a heavily fortified Jap position. And the Japs are dug in so deep in a mountain pass fortress that McLeane may have to blow the entire pass to rubble—and his men in the bargain!

#4: SAIPAN SLAUGHTER   (1510, $2.50)
Only McLeane's elite commando team had the skill—and the nerve—to go in before the invasion of Saipan and take on that key Jap stronghold. But the Japs have set a trap—which will test the jungle fighters' will to live!

Available wherever paperbacks are sold, or order direct from the Publisher. Send cover price plus 50¢ per copy for mailing and handling to Zebra Books, Dept.1610 , 475 Park Avenue South, New York, N.Y. 10016. DO NOT SEND CASH.